SNOWED IN AT THE CASTLE

SNOWED IN FOR CHRISTMAS CLEAN ROMANCE SERIES BOOK 1

LUCY MCCONNELL

ORCHARD VIEW PUBLISHING

SNOWED IN AT THE CASTLE

A light-hearted holiday romance about an orphaned woman who gets snowed in with a prince for Christmas.

What if you were snowed in far away from home with a prince...

But you thought he was just a normal guy?

A normal guy who spoke beautiful words and snuck you into the ballroom in the middle of the night just so he could hold you close?

Avery Rossi's had a rough year. She took a dream European vacation to push a restart button on her life, only to end up stranded in the airport. Her tour group is directed to temporary lodging in the castle--every girl's dream come true. When she meets a royal advisor with brooding eyes and broad shoulders, she's tempted to tear up her return ticket.

Prince Matteo de Luca must announce his engagement at the Christmas Eve ball. There are several problems.

1. The women his parents want him to marry is a troll.

2. He doesn't want to get married at all.

3. He's met an adorable American who makes him believe in things like love at first argument and the joy of Christmas.

4. She doesn't know he's a prince.

Pulled apart by centuries of tradition and loyalty to God and king, it's going to take more than a royal rebellion for these two to be together.

Find out if Christmas truly is a season for miracles in this new holiday romance today!

CLAIM YOUR FREE BOOK TODAY!

An *It Could Happen to You* retelling with a twist!

CHAPTER 1

AVERY

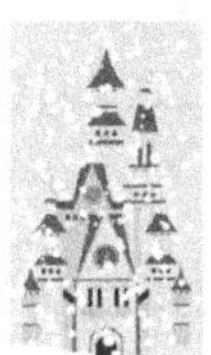

An airport, any airport, was not designed to be a gathering place. It was a shuttle from one exciting destination to the next. The fact that the seats were well used and the food was blah only made terminals suitable for short layovers. For Avery Rossi, long layovers were to be avoided if possible.

However, the small airport on Isola de la Familia was different. The floors were made of granite tile, shined and polished. The chairs were comfortable enough to lounge in, though not so lovely that one would fall asleep and miss their flight. And the temperature was regulated so that, despite the unexpectedly low winter temperatures outside, travelers could shed their coats and beanies. No one who visited the rocky shorelines, toured the stunning gardens, or tasted fruit from the local villas would expect anything less. To have a regular airport would have been an insult to the sovereign nation's reputation for refinement and beauty.

Much like the storm blowing fiercely outside was an insult to their tour guide. Sabrina waved her arms as if gathering hens into the roost. Her hair, which was usually pulled back into a low but stylish ponytail, poked out in the front as if she'd tried to dig her fingers into it in frustration.

Not a good sign.

The seven remaining travelers, who pulled into a tight circle to hear her announcement, were the free and single leftovers from their month of bebopping around Europe with 35 other adventurers. These ragtag college-aged kids carried all that they had in backpacks with too many pockets. Well, most of them. There were a couple of girls who insisted on using every inch of their space in the plane's cargo hold. Most of the group had flown out of Rome five days before —anxious to get to family and friends to celebrate the holidays.

Why would anyone from America take off the day after Thanksgiving for a pleasure tour?

Cheap flights. Cheap hotels. Less crowds. The list, which Avery's best friend had presented in an effort to get her to sign up, was longer than Santa's good list. All of it had been true too.

But it seemed their good luck had run out.

"There's good news and bad news." Sabrina lightly clasped her hands in front of her as if she wasn't worried about what she was going to say. The tightness around her eyes told a nightmare story Avery didn't want to hear.

Avery glanced down at her phone, where she'd monitored the massive snowstorm hovering off the heel of Italy. The angry red swirls covered the whole of Isola, making it difficult to discern where the land stopped and the ocean began. There was no way they were getting on a plane.

Sabrina, a native Isoladian who had shared her homeland with them over the last three days, chewed her bottom lip as she waited for ear pods to drop and phones to go dark.

Avery grabbed for Brandy's arm. Brandy was the world's best BFF. She'd been there in Avery's darkest hours and brightened many since then. The European winter tour had been her idea—a chance to make new memories instead of dwell on old ones.

"Give us the bad news first," said Brandy. A

blond beauty with a penchant for adventure, Brandy was always ready to jump out of bed to see what would happen that day. Like a puppy. Some days it was exhausting, but mostly, it was great to have a friend like that.

Sabrina twisted her hands in front of her—a sure sign that whatever was coming was bad. "We're snowed in."

Keith and Jose groaned and flopped against the back of their seats. Their skinny jeans protested the movement, crackling as if they were about to give up at the seams. They might do just that—they'd all eaten well on this trip where *diet* was a naughty word.

Greg lifted a hand as if in class. "For how long?"

Sabrina cringed. "That's the worst news. We're stuck here for a while. The storm shut down the whole island and settled in. I'm not sure when we'll get out."

Tina flew to her feet. "Will we be home for Christmas?"

Avery exchanged a look with Brandy. Tina's constant whining throughout the trip wore on the two of them like blister-causing shoes. They'd done their best to put distance between themselves and her, but with so few people left, she was hard to avoid.

"It's … unlikely. The storm is getting worse." Sabrina put up both her hands. "But there's good news. There is some really good news."

Tina crossed her arms. "Unless my nana is on a plane here with a batch of fudge, I don't want to hear it."

Despite her high-pitched sarcasm, Avery's heart went out to Tina. What she wouldn't give for one more batch of her mom's Christmas cookies.

Sabrina smiled and lifted one finger on each hand. "All right, the good news is that I have secured us a place to stay. You can all sleep in a real bed tonight and have a hot meal in the morning."

"How about a shower?" asked Stacy. She picked up her limp ponytail hanging over her shoulder and frowned at the split ends.

Avery reached back and felt her own brown messy bun. Despite the liberal amounts of dry shampoo she'd used, her hair wasn't doing her any favors. Because they were traveling, she hadn't put on any makeup either. Her hazel eyes were by far her best feature, and she'd made sure she'd had mascara on before they'd left for the airport. Hopefully, it was still on her lashes and not flaking down her cheeks.

"Showers too, because … drum roll, please … we'll be staying in a castle!" Sabrina threw her arms out and grinned. "Deluxe accommodations."

Avery's heart sank. She'd spent her savings on this trip and didn't have a cent left to her name. Her new job started in January, and she planned to eat noodles and rice until then. A room in a castle would be expensive. She glanced around, looking for a nice wall she could tuck herself against to get some shut-eye while everyone else headed off to a fairy-tale Christmas.

"What's the catch?" asked Keith with narrowed eyes. He'd pulled his hat down low, like he wanted to block out the world and whatever was happening in it.

"No catch. The owners felt bad about the situation and wanted to make sure that you all had good things to say about Isola when you left. So they offered to put you up—for *free*."

The small band around Avery's chest relaxed. She wouldn't have to stay here after all. "God bless the people who live in this castle," she said to Brandy.

"Uh, they live in a castle, so I think they're plenty blessed," Brandy quipped.

Avery smiled but didn't reply. A castle, if it wasn't a home, could be just as empty as her parents' house the day after the funeral. She braced herself for the wave of sadness such memories brought on. It came, but she was surprised that it wasn't as harsh as usual. Perhaps she was finding a new normal in life—well, as normal as it was ever going to be.

Tina squealed and did a happy dance, elated at the idea of sleeping like royalty. Keith and Jose fist-bumped. Stacy started firing questions at Sabrina about where *exactly* they'd be staying in the castle.

Sabrina waved her off. "All your questions will be answered soon, but we need to be on the move. If you'll grab your things, we'll collect the other bags at the baggage claim." Sabrina started walking backward, directing them as if she were getting a plane onto the runway. "There should be a shuttle waiting for us out front. But if we don't get there soon, the roads will be too icy and we'll have to stay the night in the airport."

Tina and Stacy broke into a trot. "Come on, people," Tina threw over her shoulder.

Avery and Brandy fell behind. Unlike everyone else, they hadn't loaded up on souvenirs that needed to be checked. Brandy's family were minimalists. You literally couldn't buy them a gift unless they could eat it. Brandy had bought a snow globe for herself in Venice, already knowing which shelf she would place it on when she got home.

Avery had splurged on one Christmas ornament in Florence at a glassblowing shop. The man there had such kind eyes, and he was a master, walking them through the process of creating art with patience and a love for his craft. She'd respected him, even felt a connection to him through the beautiful bells he created. Not a stalker kind of connection—that would be creepy —but an understanding that he put a little of his soul in every piece. His wife had packaged the ornament so carefully, and she'd promised it would survive in Avery's backpack. Still, Avery placed it on top of her expensive camera and was cautious about where she set the bag down and her clearances when she stepped through doorways.

They got to baggage claim just as everyone's boxes spewed out. Greg grabbed a rolling cart and let everyone put what they wanted on it. They went back through customs and out the sliding double doors to a waiting black van with tinted windows.

"Whoa, it's a limo van." Jose put on his sunglasses and gave the group a peace sign while Sabrina took his picture.

"I'll add it to the group photo share." She grinned at him. "Do you see how we take care of people in our country? Even visitors get the royal treatment."

The van door opened slowly, like it was done mechanically and not by the sweat of your brow like the old van Avery had grown up driving with the stained carpet and a CD player.

A driver in a green coat with silver buttons stepped around the vehicle. "*Buona giornata.*" He touched the brim of his chauffeur's hat. "You can put your bags back here, *si?*"

"*Si,*" Sabrina responded. "It's good to see you, Marco." She leaned over and kissed his cheek.

Avery giggled. "Do you think they're a thing?"

Brandy lifted a suggestive eyebrow. "How do you think we got such great *free* accommodations? Sabrina has an in at the castle."

"How lovely for us," Stacy chimed in with a smile. She was from Florida and had a difficult time adjusting to the cold temperatures. Today, she wore a tee shirt, a flannel button-up, and then a sweater under her coat. As a Midwest girl, Avery could probably last 20 minutes in the snow in just a hoodie and jeans. Stacy managed to make cold look classy, since every layer coordinated beautifully.

On the tour, conversations were rarely private. Everyone just jumped in and chatted. It was nice, like a family in a way. Avery nodded to her. "I hope so. Sabrina deserves a great guy. I've never met a nicer person."

She and Brandy settled into the middle seats, automatically leaving the back for the guys who always seemed to end up there on the train rides. Stacy took the seat in front of them. Tina was still making sure her luggage was loaded properly.

"Right?" Brandy agreed. "If they aren't a thing, we should play Christmas matchmakers."

Stacy flipped around in her seat and sighed. "I wish I could have a holiday romance." She looked over her shoulder at the guys piling in, her eyes lingering on Jose.

"Just ask him out already." Avery shoved her shoulder. "He's totally into you."

She sighed. "I don't dare. What if he says no and we're stuck together for the rest of the trip? I was trying to come up with a way to give him my cell number so we could keep in touch." She slumped. "Maybe it's just not meant to be."

"Not meant to be?" Avery echoed indignantly.

Stacy had no idea how beautiful and amazing she was—the woman was going places. Jose would be lucky to have her—if he could ever get up the nerve to ask her out. These two were so shy around each other, it was a wonder they'd every spoken at all. "You went to the same college but never met; then you end up on the same tour? Come on, there are signs here, girl."

Stacy laughed. "Okay. Maybe I'll try tonight."

"There is no try; there is only do," Brandy said in a horrible Yoda impersonation.

Avery shoulder-bumped her bestie, and they all laughed.

"What about you two?" Stacy asked them. "Anybody you want to snag before we get back home?"

Brandy bit her lip. "I wouldn't mind hanging out with Keith. But I don't think there's any future for us. He's just a good guy."

They both looked at Avery, waiting for her to profess a hidden crush. She shook her head so fast her hair whipped her face. "Forget romance, I'm just trying to get through Christmas without a meltdown. That would truly be a Christmas miracle in my book."

Both girls made that face where they cocked their heads to the side and oozed sympathy.

It grated on Avery. She'd seen way too many of those looks aimed her way in the last year. At first, they'd been welcome, but she was at a point where she wanted to move on and be strong—she just had to figure out how. "Stop it. Actually, I'm looking forward to this new adventure life threw at us. Snowed in at a castle. What could be more exciting for Christmas?"

She settled back in her seat and looked out the window at the snow that fell like spun sugar. As much as she would love to find the man of her dreams on this trip, she knew better than to make plans for life.

Because life didn't give a penny for your thoughts. Nor did it peruse your goal sheet. Nope. Life threw what it wanted at you and expected you to adapt.

That was what she was going to do. She was going to adapt to being an orphan at Christmas, and then, someday in the far future, she might be brave enough to look for love.

But not this Christmas. Certainly not this Christmas.

Nope. If there was a man out there for her, he'd just have to wait.

CHAPTER 2

MATTEO

"You must announce your engagement on Christmas Eve—it is tradition."

Matteo de Luca stared at the family portrait on the wall in his father's formal office—the king's office. Before this painting, which was presented to the king on the day his oldest son married, there was one of the oceanside that had hung there for over two hundred years. Matteo wondered where that painting had gone, as he'd liked staring at the ocean and sand much more than his older brother's success in all things pertaining to his familial duty.

Being the second son wouldn't be so bad if the first one wasn't perfect.

Padre didn't let up. "Matteo—the people are counting on you to uphold tradition. You are twenty-seven years old. This is the year of marriage for every de Luca since our family took the throne." His father stood proud, reciting history as if it were brand-new information.

It wasn't. Since the time Matteo could count to twenty-seven, he'd known that was the year he'd wed. Unfortunately for him, he also knew whom he was expected to marry, and the woman didn't make his heart race. Not that anyone besides him cared.

"Luciana has done her part well," his father continued. "You must step up and *put a ring on it, as you young ones say.*"

Matteo groaned. "Padre, please do not try to sound younger than your years."

Padre laughed from his belly. "My speechwriters say the same thing."

That's what we pay them for, Matteo thought. "Can I be honest with you?" He rarely spoke candidly with his father—it just wasn't done. They each had a role to play, and they knew their place. No one stepped out of it, even in conversation. But there were times when he was desperate to breathe.

"Please." Padre motioned for him to continue. Instead of his straight back and stiff limbs, he leaned forward, intent on Matteo.

"I do not love Luciana. And she doesn't love me." In truth, she was so sure of her place at his side that she treated him as if he were a formality in her life. Nothing more than a daily check on her to-do list. Not that he saw her daily. More like once a month at formal gatherings—if he had to attend. He was not drawn to her. There was no intrigue, no interest, nothing but a vague sense that she was all wrong for him.

Padre blinked several times. "What does that matter?"

"If I'm to spend my life with someone, I want it to be someone I want to be with. Luciana is … difficult to care for." In reality, she was a witch only lacking a broom and a pointy hat—both of which he'd be happy to gift her if she'd use them to fly out of his life forever. The thought of having children with her sent a chill down his spine that rivaled the wind hashing snow against the windows.

He continued explaining his plight. "We could cancel because of the storm. No one has seen this kind of snow in five hundred years, and no one would blame us if we put off the celebration." Matteo's hope grew as he spoke. The blizzard would shut down businesses and had already closed the airport.

Padre's face began to change color. The process was fascinating, the way the red boiled up from his starched white collar. "You would cancel the royal family's Christmas Eve celebration?" He sputtered, spit flying from his mouth. "Have you gone mad?"

It was time to put his foot down. "I cannot marry a woman I do not love."

Padre shoved his sausage finger in Matteo's face. "You will do as tradition demands. Most of the guests arrived before the storm hit, and we will proceed. This talk of love is ridiculous and not fit for a man of your station."

"On the contrary, Padre, I believe it takes a real man to insist on love in his life." He bowed slightly at the waist in goodbye and then turned smartly on his heel and left his father to sputter threats and insults behind him.

"… ungrateful … entitled …"

Matteo gritted his teeth. He had to be stronger than the forces stacked against him. He couldn't marry a woman he didn't respect, let alone like.

He wouldn't be able to look himself in the mirror on their wedding day.

No. He had to find a way out of this wedding—and fast.

CHAPTER 3

AVERY

"The servants' quarters?" Tina shrieked loud enough that the coat of arms hanging on the wall shook. "This just won't do."

Avery looked around for a closet to hide in or a sofa to duck behind so she would be out of Tina's way should she throw herself to the floor kicking and screaming.

A hiding spot didn't magically appear, but there were boughs of holly draped along each wall, creating a homey feeling. A Christmas tree stood in the center of the gathering room. Each ornament had a name on it, which Sabrina told them was a tradition. The royal family had an ornament made for each of the staff members every year. They could keep them as a memento of their time spent in service in the castle. They were quite beautiful and rivaled the one Avery had purchased in Venice. "It must cost them a fortune," she'd commented.

Sabrina had smiled indulgently. "The de Luca family is known for their generosity to the people who work for them. Because they serve the people of Isola, they understand what it means to spend your time for another. Some families pass the jobs down; they have over a hundred years' worth of ornaments."

Avery liked the idea of a royal family who cared about everyone—down to the last servant hired. She'd touched a glass ball, spinning it around to find the royal crest on the back. "Stunning," she'd whispered.

Her quiet thoughts were interrupted by a man's sarcastic remark to Tina's demands. "Would you prefer that I ask the queen to vacate the royal suite so you can move in?" asked the rather large and imposing butler-ish man wearing a full tuxedo in the middle of the afternoon. He had a way of looking down his nose at them without lifting his chin.

"Can you do that?" Tina bounced on her toes. "I already brag-posted about sleeping here, and that would make some excellent—"

"No, *ragazza,* I will not ask the queen to leave her bed." At this, he did lift his chin and glared down his rather impressive nose.

Avery hid her giggle behind her hand. He'd basically called Tina *missy,* and she didn't catch it —although her face fell into an impressive pout because she wouldn't be sleeping in the royal suite.

"Come on." Brandy hooked Avery's elbow. "Let's claim a room before everyone else. I don't want to get stuck next to Greg." She made a snoring noise that rivaled lumberjacks taking down trees back home.

Avery went willingly. "Let's get the one at the end. That way we won't have to share both walls."

"Good idea. But …" Brandy looked over her shoulder. "I think the bathroom is that way." The gathering room was the center of a set of hallways set out like spokes. Sabrina had given them a quick history of the castle as they'd driven up the switchbacks leading to the main entrance, which they'd bypassed to go around to the back, where they unloaded at the servants' area. When the castle had been constructed, indoor plumbing wasn't a glimmer in the eye of the king, and the castle had had to be retrofitted —not an easy task, and one that left many exposed pipes that couldn't be hidden inside the thick block walls.

Avery brushed her off. "We're not old yet—our bladders will survive a few extra steps."

They picked a room and unpacked pajamas and toothbrushes, not sure how long they'd be staying and not wanting to settle in too much.

Sabrina wandered up and down the hall, making sure everyone was situated. "I'm working on getting us a tour of the castle. They're really busy with the Christmas Eve celebration, but hopefully we'll have permission soon."

Avery laid back on her bed. The sheets were better quality than the ones she slept in at home, and the mattress … "What is this made of, angel wings?" She rubbed her hands over the soft blanket.

Brandy threw her arms above her head and wiggled deeper. "I could sleep for days."

Avery rolled onto her stomach and propped her chin on her fist. "Not me. This is my first sleepover in a castle—a royal castle to boot. I'm going back to the gathering room to take some pictures of the tree and such." She might never get the chance to be this deep in a royal anything ever again. She wanted proof.

Brandy flicked a hand in goodbye. "Let me

know if you find anything worth getting up for, will you?"

"Sure." Avery stepped into the hall. They had the last door in the hallway. To her right was a bookshelf, thick and full of leather and fabric-bound beauties. "Those can't be real." She headed that direction, assuming she'd reach her hand out to touch a painting or some kind of wallpaper or mural. Instead, she brushed her fingers over cold leather and gasped.

Tipping her head, she read titles out loud—well, the ones she could pronounce, anyway. Many of them were in Italian and … was that German? "*La Divina Commedia … Orlando Furioso … I Promessi Sposi.*" She paused after the last one. "The Betrothed. *Hmm.*" She reached up to pull the book off the shelf, only to have it stick in place. "Strange." Her finger clearly hooked over the spine. She tugged a little harder, and the bookshelf clicked.

The bookshelf. *Clicked.*

"What in the world?" She pushed the book back in place, and the whole wall swung in. "Oh no, I broke the castle." Panic rushed through her as she looked over her shoulder. Sabrina was going to kill her.

Her breath came in sharply. She tried to pull

the hidden door back in place, but the darn thing wouldn't budge. Music started loudly from one of the rooms down the hall, and she jumped in surprise. "Shoot." Ducking onto the other side of the shelf, she shoved, not even bothering to see what was on this side. She prayed it wasn't a den of spiders. She shuddered. She hated spiders.

Frantically looking for a lever of some kind, she saw the same set of books on this side as was on the other and reached for *I Promessi Sposi.* Tugging the spine, she was yanked off balance as the shelf threw itself back in place. Her body ended up smacking into the bookcase and rattling the gold vase at the top.

"Ow." She rubbed her sore spots, waiting to see if anything fell or broke, but it all stayed in place. Relief was like a warm cup of cocoa on a cold winter day. "Whew." She stepped back and brushed off her palms. It was only then that she realized she was on the wrong side of the door. Glaring at the books, she put her hands on her hips while she debated going back through. If the door didn't shut this time, she'd have to tell someone.

"You there!"

She jumped in fright and spun around to find a terribly handsome man striding her way. "You scared the Dickens out of me." She almost smiled, thinking of how her Dad used to say that all the time. It was neat that they were still with her, a part of her life in so many ways. She should thank this guy for helping her find one more of her parents' quirks they'd passed on.

Only … She couldn't seem to get her tongue to work. It was paralyzed by the massive amounts of gorgeousness in front of her.

He wore a dark brown sweater that went perfectly with his true brown hair—so typical of this region. Where many of the Italians she'd met on the mainland had black or sable hair, this man's was lighter but more forest-y. His eyes were dark green. He loomed over her, his face dark and dangerous, his stature one of importance. Despite the fact that she'd just come through a hidden bookcase in a castle older than her country, all she could think about was how handsome he was. It was as if her brain had stayed behind the bookshelves. Maybe it had, because she blurted, "You have a perfect nose. Truly, I've never seen its equal." She froze, ready to smack herself in the forehead. Who says that?

He stopped in his tracks and regarded her cautiously. "Are you right in the head?"

"Am I—" She stopped, the insult hitting its

mark, expertly delivered by the derision dripping from his voice.

She was not *right in the head;* she was all fuzzy and twitterpated over his gorgeousness. However, other than being knocked off her good sense, she was mentally stable. He should be used to this kind of reaction—after all, he was the picture of perfection. Surely women had lost their heads over him before.

Not that he needed to know that he had that effect on her. "Of course I am. Are you?"

"Yes," he replied slowly, his eyes roaming over her as if looking for some proof that she hadn't escaped from a loony bin. She glanced down at her skinny jeans and creamy sweater, then back up at him, silently asking if he was done checking her out.

He made a small sound, something like a *pst* that said, *I would not lower myself to date a woman in no-name jeans.*

She rolled her eyes. He was too much. Too much handsome and too full of himself. Thank goodness for his superiority complex—it was quite the turnoff. "If you're done ogling me, you can get back to whatever you were doing before."

Wow, she was not good at this whole witty banter thing. That came out more snobby than cute and funny. Sheesh. She was out of practice in the flirting department. Better to make her escape than stand here and humiliate herself any more. She turned to leave and sucked in a breath.

He sputtered a response behind her, but she tuned him out, because she'd just noticed the room. It was magnificent! Gleaming wood paneling covered the walls. In each panel was a beehive with busy little occupants going about their business. Maroon fabric wallpaper coated the areas that wood didn't cover as well as the two couches arranged facing one another. A large picture window looked out over a snow-covered garden. The scene was artist worthy. Giant flakes continued to fall—even larger than they'd been when she'd arrived.

She continued her slow perusal only to circle back to the grumpy man, who studied her as intently as she'd studied the space. He'd finally gone quiet, which seemed like a rare state for him.

Taking advantage of his momentary silence, she decided to go right past him; there was no way she'd unlock the secret passageway with this guy staring at her. He might accuse her of bringing the whole castle down upon them. If she looked like she knew where she was going, then he'd leave her alone, right?

She started off at a quick pace—intent on escaping her horrible behavior.

To her chagrin, he dodged her steps. "I'm sorry, who are you?"

"No need to apologize," she said flippantly as she tried her best to brush him off. *Just keep walking like you have business in the castle.*

He wasn't having any of her false confidence. "I wasn't apologizing. What I should have said was: Excuse me, what do you think you're doing wandering around the castle?"

She bit her lip. She shouldn't be where she was, but she didn't know how to get back to where she was going. And she didn't want to get Sabrina in trouble. Whatever strings the tour guide had pulled to get them angel-winged mattresses and free rooms, they probably weren't strong enough to stand up under Avery's ability to muck things up.

But if there was one thing she'd learned over the last year, it was to fake it until she made it. Squaring her shoulders, she stopped just outside of another long hallway and looked her shadow man right in the face. Which turned out to be a mistake of gargantuan proportions, because he looked even better when he wasn't scowling. He was the kind of handsome that took her breath away and allowed her traitorous knees to grow weak.

She gathered all of her mental abilities and borrowed some of Tina's attitude and asked hotly, "Who are you, the castle police?" She meant the words to be demanding and forceful, but they came out breathy and flirty because he was in her personal space and he smelled like manliness—all spicy and woodsy and *mmm*.

He lifted a condescending brow. "No. That would be the guards. You will recognize them because they wear uniforms."

She wanted to get back to her room right this minute, to hide under her pillow until the airport opened and she could go home where there weren't beautiful men following her around and demanding answers she didn't have. "Then what do you care who I am and where I go?"

He sighed a long-suffering sigh. "You're obviously lost, as this is the private wing of the castle reserved for the royal family and a few select staff members, and I'd like to help you find your way."

"Oh." Shoot. "Why didn't you say so in the first place instead of acting accusatory and grumpy?"

He tipped his head. "I'm not grumpy."

"Yes, you are." She pointed to the line between his brow. "You're wrinkling in all the grumpy places."

His hand flew to the line and his eyes went wide as he realized she was right. "My apologies, *signorina*. I've had a trying conversation with the king and must have brought some of his grumpy along with me."

"The king?" *The king!* This guy spoke to the king. She looked around quickly, expecting his royal highness to appear behind him. "I've stepped in it now, haven't I?"

He glanced down at her shoes and sniffed.

It took her a moment to realize he was teasing her. The humor was dry and understated, but there nonetheless. The teasing, paired with his slight smile, did funny things to her stomach. She swatted his arm. "Stop it. I didn't actually step in anything." Suddenly realizing that she'd sort of, maybe just flirted with this guy, she schooled herself. "I'm with a tour group that was stranded at the airport, and I lost my way." She waved her hand around, indicating the general building.

"Sabrina's group?" His forehead wrinkled in a totally different way than it had when he was worried because of a conversation with the king.

This was adorable, like he was putting a puzzle together.

Oh no, she'd done it now—throwing Sabrina under the bus. She shouldn't have said anything. She held her breath, waiting for trouble to start. "Don't be mad at her. I'm the one who wandered off—by accident, I promise. Wait, how do you know Sabrina?" He'd used her first name. And he knew they were in the servants' quarters below the stairs. That was a lot of insider information, and it made her wonder what was going on. Should she be jealous of her tour guide? Maybe Marco the driver wasn't the one sneaking kisses under the mistletoe.

"She's a cousin," he replied.

The green-eyed monster let go of her chest, and she slouched in relief. "Oh—so you, like, work here?"

Something passed behind his eyes—regret? Sadness? Resignation? She couldn't quite put a name to it. "Every day of my life."

"I heard about families like yours. I think it's neat that you take pride in what you do and pass down the job. I mean, it's a beautiful heritage that not everyone can lay claim to."

He regarded her deeply.

"What?" She brushed her cheek, wondering if

she'd left crumbs there from the awful muffin she'd eaten at the airport.

"I argued with my padre earlier about that very thing—a son's obligation. It is interesting that you brought it up as well."

"Oh." She tucked her hair behind her ear and ducked her face, feeling as though she'd jumped into a family squabble. "I'm sorry. I didn't mean to, you know, intrude."

He hooked his finger under her chin, the contact making her heart thrum. "Thank you for reminding me that familial obligations are not always a burden."

She wrinkled her forehead and grunted. "Family isn't a burden; it's a blessing." One she would gladly have back.

He smiled. "You are certainly American."

"I'm taking that as a compliment."

He laughed. "I didn't mean it any other way." He offered his arm. "Please, allow me to escort you back to your quarters."

She looked at his elbow, which he held out like he was some knight in shining armor. Wow— the castle must be working its magic on her. The next thing she knew, she'd be challenging someone to a duel. If the prize was a kiss from this guy, she might just take up a sword. "Okay, but if you take me to the dungeon and lock me up, I swear I will haunt this place for all time." There! She'd finally remembered how to tease a good-looking man. Whew! For a while there, she'd thought she was broken beyond repair.

"I've known you for ten minutes and would expect nothing less."

"Okay, then, as long as we're on the same page." She slipped her hand in his arm, feeling princess-ish and cherished and all sorts of things she hadn't felt in a long time. He stood so tall, so straight. She found herself sucking in and following his lead. His long legs and determined stride were an effort to keep up with—and she'd been walking all over Europe for four weeks. "Are you always in a hurry?"

He immediately slowed down. "Usually, yes. But I thought it was best to get you out of the prince regent's private quarters before someone saw you."

Her mind raced. There was a secret passage between the servants' quarters and the prince's home. *Hmm.* Either someone in history had had a scandalous love affair, or they were serious about the help not being seen. With the passageway, cleaning the royal chambers would be easy. She did her best to put the whole thing out of her mind. She wouldn't be using the passageway again—especially knowing it went to the prince's apartment. "He's the married prince, right?"

"Si."

"I guess it wouldn't do to have a strange woman wandering around his apartment, then. Sabrina gave us an overview of the royal family when we got here." She craned her neck to take in the paintings of cherubs on the ceiling in a grand hall of some sort. "I should have paid more attention."

He stopped at a small door that had several inlays and patterns. The knob had a beehive on it.

"What with the bees?" she asked, pointing.

He glanced down and then started as if he hadn't ever seen the design before. Which was strange, because the wear on the knob indicated it was older than she was. "Our island is home to a special strain of honeybee that is coveted the world over. Our bees travel across Europe to help with many crops—from blueberries to orange trees. They're especially good pollinators."

She giggled. When he kept his stony face, she sobered up. "Sorry. You sounded like a Wikipedia article for a minute there."

He swallowed as if trying to maintain his composure. Had she really gotten to him, almost made him laugh? Seeing his smile felt like a challenge—one she would gladly accept if she was ever going to see him again.

"This is the door to the servants' quarters. You can find your group from here, I assume?"

"You assume correctly." She smiled and stuck out her hand. "It's been nice meeting you, Jeeves. If you don't cut it as a butler, I'm sure you'll make a great tour guide."

He took her hand in his, slowly sliding his fingers across her palm before gripping her hand. The heat that shot up her arm made her cheeks blush. "Your compliment overwhelms me."

There went his dry humor again. When it was directed at her, she had a hard time maintaining brain waves. Her blush turned to a full flush. "I'm just going to … um … bye." She popped through the servants' door—which was not labeled and looked just as beautiful as any door she'd seen in the rest of the castle. It shut quietly behind her, and she looked down the long hallway to see the Christmas tree at the center of the spokes. Her group had gathered around, and she was missing whatever announcement Sabrina was dishing up.

Goodness, she'd have to figure out which spokes to avoid and which ones were allowed. If only they'd labelled things. It wasn't like she was a complete idiot; she could read a sign—if there was one.

"Avery!" Brandy hissed and waved for her to hurry.

She jogged over, hoping her crew would attribute the color on her cheeks to the physical exertion and not to the fact that she'd just met a very stuffy—but good-looking—butler.

"… not getting out by Christmas Eve." Sabrina had a screen in the crook of her arm. "However, I have been instructed by the royal family to keep you all entertained and given a pass to some areas of the castle that may prove to be a diversion."

"Where were you?" Brandy asked, using Jose as a block between her and Sabrina so the tour guide wouldn't know they were chatting.

"I got lost."

"It's, like, five hallways!"

"I know," Avery whispered, and then she clamped her mouth shut. She was about to tell Brandy about Jeeves, but something made her hold back. The idea that she could get in a lot of trouble definitely had something to do with it— not that Brandy would sell her out or anything. She glanced down the other hallways and made note of where the bookshelf sat and where this hallway with its door into the castle proper was located.

Maybe she'd bump into the butler again as they were entertained by the royal family.

Yeah, and maybe she'd wake up a princess on Christmas morning.

CHAPTER 4

MATTEO

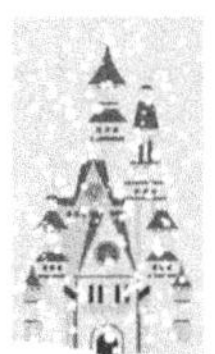

The snow continued to build up around the castle in great mounds. The local plows and road service crews worked around the clock to keep businesses open, since it was the week before Christmas. The economy counted on this week to sustain small companies.

Matteo stayed in contact with the senator over transportation, requesting hourly updates. He didn't have good things to say. "Snow is in the forecast for the next four days. We'll be lucky to dig ourselves out."

Matteo took his concerns to heart, but he couldn't take in his cynicism. Snow was part of the weather, after all, and it always changed. Eventually, spring would come.

However, the forecast called for heavy snows right up to Christmas Day. They'd be lucky to get the airport open on the holiday, and there were many people stranded in Isola hotels and bed and breakfasts who would not make it home to toast Christ's birth with their families. What's more, shopping was limited, which meant the economy was going to suffer.

"I understand." Matteo kept his face impassive. "But unlike the Americans and their Black Friday shopping in November, Isoladians put off Christmas shopping until the week before. Our people need clear roads and open businesses." He mentally berated himself. He'd been thinking about America and a certain brown-haired, hazel-eyed American in particular all morning. The way she'd defended families was noble. He wondered what had put such a strong fight in her soul.

"*Si, principe.* We will make stores and shopping a priority. *Gratzie.*" The senator bowed his head, revealing the thinning hair on top, and the screen went dark.

Matteo twirled his pen around his thumb—an old habit from his school days when he had a difficult math problem to solve.

"*Signore?*" Alfredo, his personal steward, set a

cup of herbal tea on the table. "Is there something on your mind?"

"No," he answered absently.

"Perhaps it is the upcoming ball and finalizing the place settings?" Alfredo prompted.

Matteo sighed a do-I-have-to sigh—also a leftover from his school days. "*Ottimo*, very well." He stood, allowing Alfredo to show him to the sideboard, where three place settings were laid out. One was white, one was red, and one had holly leaves around the edges. "The holly. It's a Christmas Eve celebration, after all. We should look festive."

Alfredo frowned.

"What?"

"It's the same setting your brother used when he announced his proposal."

"Is that a problem? Pedro always wished I was more like Angelo; what better place to start than with the dishes?" His joke fell flat against the stodgy older man. He had a feeling the girl in the hallway who admired his nose would have liked it. She seemed to have his same sense of humor— dry as the sands, as his madre would say.

He actually found her quite fun to tease—in a small way. Truly, finding her standing in his brother's library had been the most interesting thing to happen to him in years. He'd almost forbidden her from leaving, but she'd ducked away so quickly he hadn't stood a chance. It wasn't like a prince could go chasing a woman into the servants' quarters—there were rules to follow when it came to decorum.

Decorum: another thing his padre thought he lacked in. Wouldn't Padre be proud of his refrain yesterday?

She'd called him Jeeves. He'd looked up the name and found that it was a reference to a butler. She thought he was a butler. Either she was an excellent con artist who was playing an elaborate game, or she had no idea he was a prince. Which was kind of funny, considering she was staying in his castle. A person should know their host. He wished she was here right now so he could point that out and see what her reply would be. No doubt she'd keep him on his toes.

"*Principe*, if I may suggest the red. You always seem to have a flair for the dramatic, and it would make the statement that you are your own man."

Matteo turned to look at him. "If that was the right choice, why didn't you just say so?"

"A man should know his options, *principe*. And what good does it do to make the right choice if I make it for you?" He pushed his chin out, elongating his neck as if accenting his words.

"You are right, old friend." Matteo looked them over once again. The red setting was bold. But the white? It held a freshness to it—a sense of a new beginning. "I'd like the white—it's like a clean slate. A chance to write my own way in the world."

Alfredo smiled and bowed as much as his arthritic hip would allow. "Now you are thinking like a prince."

"No, friend. Now I am thinking like a man." Perhaps too much like a man, as his thoughts were constantly spinning around a *signorina* who was lost in more way than one. He'd seen it in her eyes, a reflection of his own search to find his place in the world. "Tell me, what do you know of the tourists we took in? Are they comfortable?"

If Alfredo was surprised by the turn in the conversation, he didn't show it. The man was a veritable statue. When Matteo was a child, he used to imagine that at Alfredo's death, they would simply wheel him out to the garden and set him among the pelargoniums. He was a rather morbid child, come to think of it.

"They are as comfortable as can be expected

when displaced from their homes. They have food and a warm place to sleep."

He thought of the warmth in the young woman's hazel eyes. Simply comfortable wouldn't do. "Allow them access to the bowling alley for a night. Let them have some fun."

Alfredo narrowed his eyes. "That's for family use only."

"It's Christmas." Matteo clapped him on the shoulder, and Alfredo coughed as if he'd knocked the wind out of him. "They are far from home. We can well afford one night of revelry for our guests."

Alfredo considered him a moment. "*Ottimo,* very well."

Matteo smiled and went back to his desk to look over the budget for snow removal. As he sat there, his mind wandered back to the library and the *signorina* with the stunning hazel eyes and full lips that held his attention for all the wrong reasons.

CHAPTER 5

AVERY

"I can't believe they're letting us into the family's private chambers."

Avery suppressed her smile and the urge to blurt out that she'd already been there. Been there, ticked off the butler, but didn't get a tee shirt. She was totally going to make herself that tee shirt when she got home. She'd earned it. And if wearing it reminded her of the grumpy butler who made her heart race, then so be it.

Brandy grabbed her arm and shook it. "It's just so exciting. I wish we didn't have to leave our phones behind, though."

Tina growled. "If it wasn't the chance of a lifetime, I would have flat-out refused." She'd spent the last half hour spraying something in her hair that smelled like coconuts and made it shinier than the Christmas lights twinkling around the castle. When asked, she replied that you never knew who you were going to run into in a castle. There was one Isoladian prince who was single and looking for a princess. Then she'd lifted a shoulder as if to say, *Why not me?*

"I thought they were going to have to get out a scalpel to separate your phone from you hand," Avery teased.

"Har har." Tina took it all in good fun. "Sabrina said no one but the royal family and the cleaning staff has seen the bowling alley. What if we end up bowling with the king? Wouldn't that be sick?"

"I'd rather meet a butler." Avery closed her eyes in regret the moment the words were out.

"A butler?" Stacy laughed, joining in the conversation. "What's so good about a butler?"

Avery grinned. They'd change their minds pretty quickly if they saw the butler she'd seen. "Well, for one, they know their way around a kitchen."

"They do?" Stacy walked backward, her hand on Jose's shoulder so she didn't run into anything. She still hadn't gotten his number, but they had rooms next to each other and realized they liked the same grunge band. So at least they were talking. Jose didn't turn to join in. Maybe he was happy to be right where he was, within touching distance of Stacy, and didn't want to move in case she pulled her hand away.

It was possible that Avery had started seeing romance everywhere after her encounter with *Jeeves*. She may also have had several imaginary dream dates with said butler before she'd fallen asleep last night. But she couldn't drop back into her imagination right now. She had to stay focused on the path they took to the bowling alley so she'd know her way around if she ever got lost again.

Brandy's mouth dropped open. "Butlers are head of the kitchen and dining staff. Don't you ever watch British shows?"

"Rarely." Stacy flipped around and put her arm though Jose's. For a girl who was too shy to give him her number, she'd upped her game.

Avery exchanged a look with Brandy, and they hid their giggles behind their hands. "I'm proud of her," Avery said. "She sees what she wants, and she's going for it."

Brandy nodded. "Does that mean you've figured out what to do with your life? That job offer is dangling in your email."

Avery groaned. She'd finished up an internship right before the trip. They'd offered her a position, but she'd told them she wouldn't decide until they got back. "I'm taking the job."

Brandy deflated. "Yeah, but only because you have to have a job. You're not passionate about product development."

She wasn't. But with her degree, it made sense, and this job had sort of fallen in her lap. "It's something until I find my passion."

"You mean rediscover it. Ever since the accident, it's like you're empty inside. Which is totally understandable. I would be too if both my parents passed away. I just hoped this trip would put some life back in you."

Avery thought back to her encounter with Jeeves. She'd felt something with him—warm and alive. Real. Almost … like herself again. Grief had hollowed her out, but talking with Jeeves made her feel solid. "I think I'm on the right path," she said slowly. "I'm finding parts of myself every day. Who knew they'd be scattered over Europe? Being here—" She glanced around at the beautiful architecture and stunning furniture. "—has helped. Thank you for twisting my arm until I came."

Brandy gave her a side hug. "That's what friends do."

They walked through a set of double doors. One thing Avery noticed was that any entry meant for the royal family was made up of double doors. Servants only had one door, which was weird, but it helped her know where she should and shouldn't go. The bowling alley was made for the royal family's entertainment, so it had a double-door entry.

Inside, the walls were painted dark blue and neon lights lit up four alleys.

"Would you look at this place?" Keith threw his arms out to the side and crowed like a rooster.

Sabrina gave him a dirty look. "A little class, *Signore* Wormwood, if you please."

He winked at her. "Anything for you, darlin'."

Brandy rolled her eyes at his antics. "His accent isn't that thick—he's just playing the redneck from Arkansas because he thinks it's cute."

Avery bumped her with her hip. "*You* think it's kind of cute—don't ya?"

Brandy dissolved into giggles. "Maybe a little. I've always enjoyed a Southern man's vernacular," she said in her own Southern twang. She'd lived in the South until she was ten and then moved to

Montana, where she and Avery became best friends forever—at least, that was what their matching bracelets said.

They all found shoes on the shelf and balls on the rack, and they figured out how to put their names into the computer that projected their scores overhead for the whole world to see. Well, everyone in the room. Avery wasn't the worst player; that spot was reserved for Greg. His surfer looks were popular with the ladies, and he'd had his share of tour romances, sweeping local girls off their feet in a night and stealing a kiss before the tour moved on. He kept trying to put a professional spin on the ball and ended up in the gutter.

"One of these times I'm gonna get it just right," he said as he flopped into the chair next to Avery.

"Sure." Avery patted his arm.

"So Sabrina, what's the chances of a prince coming down here tonight?" Stacy tossed her ball. It landed with a *thunk* before slowly rolling into the gutter.

Sabrina folded her arms. "No chance. The royal family is preparing for the Christmas Eve ball. They are too busy to bowl."

"Isn't he getting married on Christmas Eve?"

asked Greg. Throughout the trip, he surprised them all with odd tidbits of knowledge.

"Engaged," Sabrina corrected him.

"To who?" asked Stacy. She wasn't at all worried that her second ball rolled slower than a caterpillar.

"Luciana something."

"But there's talk that it might not go through," Greg threw out as if tossing a juicy piece of meat into a lion's den.

Tina snatched it up. "Really? Why not?"

Avery flicked her gaze to Sabrina to see if she would refute the gossip. Sabrina pressed her red lips together and looked the other way.

Jeeves would know what was going on behind double doors. He lived with the royal family—as close as any staff member could be, having access to their private living quarters. Maybe he'd shared some news with his cousin and she wasn't allowed to repeat it.

"They're rarely seen together, and when they are—there's no chemistry," Greg finished.

"Arranged marriages are often like that," Sabrina finally spoke up.

"It sounds lonely," Avery blurted. She glanced down at her hands in her lap. She knew loneliness, the kind that entered your soul like an unwelcome guest when everyone you loved vacated the premises. She didn't wish that on anyone. "I feel bad for him—for both of them. A family should be full of love, not obligation or politics. It's the one place in the world where you should be accepted just the way you are." That was how she'd been raised—by two of the most loving people ever created by God. He'd made them perfect—too perfect to stay on this earth longer than it took to raise her. Then he took them home.

Brandy touched her arm, bringing her out of her musings.

"Well, I think it sounds romantic. A ball. A gown. A proposal in front of your friends and family." Stacy swooned and landed in her chair with her hand to her forehead. She sat up. "I don't even have to be a princess—I just want to go."

Sabrina chuckled. "Keep dreaming, Cinderella. The guest list was written over a year ago. Most of the attendees are royalty or influential Isoladians or from neighboring countries. We're staying downstairs, remember?"

Stacy scowled and sat up.

"I'd rather spend Christmas with my family." Tina made her way to the ball return. She looked over her shoulder. "But if a prince asked me to the ball, I wouldn't say no. It sounds like the perfect Christmas to me." She winked at them and then set herself to throw a strike.

They all cheered as the pins fell. She was in the lead, much to Greg's dismay.

Brandy leaned over Avery to encourage him. "Don't worry. As soon as you perfect that spin, you'll take the lead." She hopped up to take her turn.

Avery stared at the floor. What would the perfect Christmas look like? For her, it wouldn't be at a ball. It would be in her mom's kitchen making sugar cookies, or building a snow man with her dad. He insisted on having one every year. She'd thought it was so silly, and now? She'd give anything to build one with him again.

"Does anyone feel like building a snowman tomorrow?" she asked.

Keith laughed. "Yeah, I'm not going outside in this weather. Girl, I'm from SoCal. We don't do snow."

She smiled easily. His answer wasn't a shock. "How about you guys?" she asked Jose and Stacy.

They shook their heads. "No thanks. I'm good." Jose threw his arm behind Stacy's chair.

Stacy angled herself so she leaned against him. "Me too. Thanks, though."

Avery glanced at the people around her, smiling as if it wasn't a big deal. This wasn't what she'd planned for her life—heck, it wasn't what she'd planned for this Christmas. But being stranded in a castle might be a gift from God, because it took her out of her grief and planted her in a new place. A palace, actually. And she wasn't so sad here without the reminders all around. Really, it was a blessing.

But that didn't mean she couldn't keep them alive in her heart. She'd build a snowman … as soon as she figured out how to get out of the castle. And if she could run into a certain butler again, she might just enjoy flirting with him.

CHAPTER 6

MATTEO

"I'm afraid Madre's sense of humor has gotten the best of her this year." Matteo looked down at the cream-colored sweater with a giant reindeer face on the front, bells hanging from the antlers. "I jingle when I walk."

"It's a monstrosity," agreed his older brother, Angelo, as he drew an equally disturbing sweater over his head. His was also cream, but with a snowman in a red plaid vest. He looked down and made a face. "The things we do for women."

Matteo laughed.

Angelo pointed at him. "Laugh all you want—your time is coming."

Matteo sobered. "What if I didn't get married this year?"

"Then the whole country would fall to ruin." Angelo combed his fingers through his hair, the same color as Matteo's, working to get it to lie just right. Royal family portraits were a big deal, but this one was special. Madre never allowed the public to see their informal holiday photos. They were family memories kept close and cherished. Hence the reason they could wear goofy sweaters.

"You don't believe that, do you?" Matteo checked his reflection. His hair had grown over his ears and had a soft wave. He rather liked the unkempt look—so did the press. They thought his bad-boy image was an improvement over his clean-cut look. One article remarked that he was the bad boy of Isola with his reputation for dating every available woman on the island. But frequent dates with other women were a shield against Luciana, who would have his social calendar linked to her phone so she could keep him all to herself. If only he liked her, just a little.

"I don't. But I believe in duty and honor—they both bring good things. If you do your part, the country will continue on as it has for hundreds of years. If you don't, there are … hiccups."

"We can't have hiccups," Matteo grumbled.

Angelo gave himself a final look. "No, we

can't." He headed for the hallway. "I'm going to get my family. I'll meet you in the main hall."

Matteo grumbled his way to the hall where the family would converge for pictures. "Do my part … hiccups … like he's ever had hiccups … Prince Angel who always does as he's told …"

His sour mood was interrupted by his two much younger sisters. He and Angelo used to joke that Madre and Padre had two boys out of obligation and then the girls out of love. It probably took that long for them to really care about one another. Although it was nice to know that his parents had developed a love to stand the test of time, Matteo remembered the years of cold indifference and formal interactions that made up his childhood. It was a frigid way to grow up, though both his parents loved him individually.

"Well, if it isn't the two prettiest monsters in the castle." Matteo scooped them both in for hugs.

Carlotta was ten and Emmilia nine. They were carbon copies—practically twins—except for their height. Their sable-brown hair hung in waves down to the middle of their backs. Their cream sweaters had gingerbread men on them, one with a red scarf and one with a green scarf. If they didn't like each other so much, they'd hate dressing alike. But they were the best of friends, often finishing one another's sentences. And they were the darlings of the whole country—beloved by all.

But no one doted on them more than Matteo.

"I believe one must be a monster to recognize a monster," Carlotta teased as she pecked a kiss to his cheek.

"Well, we are related," Matteo countered. He nodded to their nanny that he'd take the girls from here, and she melted into the library. The woman loved reading more than breathing. That was one of the reasons Madre had chosen her as an influence in the girls' lives. She'd passed that love on to the girls. Matteo couldn't wait to give them their Christmas gifts--autographed books from their favorite authors.

They each took one of his hands and swung them as they continued their walk together.

"Have you been out in the snow yet?" he asked.

Emmilia shook her head and frowned. *"Bambinaia* says we can't go out until tomorrow."

"We're simply booked with fittings and dance lessons for the ball," added Carlotta.

"You are? Well, let's see how those lessons are

paying off." He dropped Emmilia's hand and took up Carlotta in a waltzing position. She giggled as he took large steps, making it difficult for her to keep up.

Emmilia laughed behind them. "That's what she looks like in class."

Carlotta threw her a dirty look. "I'd like to see you dance with this giraffe."

Matteo spun her around and then waltzed her right into the grand hall. "A giraffe, *si?*"

All joking and teasing thoughts flew from his mind as his eyes focused on a pretty American decorating their Christmas tree. No, she wasn't decorating; she was re-decorating, taking ornaments off one place and putting them in another.

The girls paused to watch. They looked at him for an explanation. He shrugged.

Matteo's heart began a steady, deep beat. He'd hoped to run into her again, but then decided it was best if he didn't. Apparently, fate or Christmas sprites had other ideas.

"What are you doing?" asked Emmilia. Her childlike voice filled the room. A large, ornate carpet would be rolled across the floor to help absorb sound the night of the ball as guests entered and greeted one another. But tonight, the floor was bare and sound echoed off every space.

The stranger's face lit up as she took in the two girls by his side. At least, he gave credit to his sisters. There was no way she was that happy to see him—not after the abysmal way he'd behaved the last time they'd spoken. "I'm fixing this tree," she replied. Having struck a chord of curiosity in all of them—perhaps intentional, but most likely not—she went back to work.

Matteo looked down at his sisters, and they all then stepped forward together. "But what's wrong with it?" asked Carlotta.

"Well …" She stepped back and surveyed her work. "The baubles should be deeper in the branches, where they can catch the lights. And the crests should be toward the ends of the branches, where they can be admired without having to stick you face in the pine needles."

The image of her pushing her face into the tree to get a better look made Matteo break into a grin. "I'm guessing you learned of this defect from experience."

She blushed and ran her finger over her cheek, just under her eye. "Maybe."

"You should be more careful when observing Christmas trees. The pastime can be quite dangerous for the inexperienced." He held his breath, hoping she would take his reprimand for the joke he meant it to be.

Her eyes twinkled. Before she could respond, Carlotta elbowed him in the stomach. "Don't be rude to our guest." She rolled her eyes as if she were five years older than him. "I'm Carlotta. This is my sister, Emmilia, and my older and most apologetic brother, Matteo."

"Avery," she replied, putting her hand out. The girls shook her hand and smiled. When she got to Matteo, her face flushed. "It's a pleasure to officially meet you."

"You can call me Jeeves." He continued to hold her hand, pressing it between both of his as if he'd come upon a long-lost friend. Because that was the feeling that swelled inside of his chest. *You know her*, it whispered.

"I think I like Matteo better." She glanced down, and her long lashes rested against her cheeks in a most fascinating way. It was like watching a kitten fall asleep.

"You are American?" Emmilia noted.

"Shh." Carlotta put a finger over her mouth. "I'm sorry. We just weren't expecting … you," she finished lamely.

Avery laughed easily. "I wasn't expecting to be

here either—I got lost on my way outside to build a snowman." Her gaze turned back to the tree. "This may be the only tree I get to decorate this year. I hope you don't mind."

"Won't your family decorate one?" Carlotta demurely folded her hands together in front of her. She would make an excellent queen one day. Unlike Matteo, her marriage had yet to be decided. In all likelihood, the girls would be free to choose their own spouses—far from the pressures he faced.

Avery's face dipped with sadness. "I'm sort of floating on my own this year without our traditions."

A feeling of protection raised up inside of Matteo—one he hadn't known existed. He wanted to gather her close and wipe the grimness from her life. The most astonishing thing about the feeling was that it was all about taking care of her, and he didn't mind one bit. With as much as he fought against the expectations hanging on him like a bridle on a horse, having a desire to care for her was refreshing.

"Well, we can't have that," announced Carlotta.

"What traditions did you do?" pressed Emmilia.

Matteo's heart grew for his sisters. They too wanted to make Christmas special for this woman they'd just met. Unlike him, they were inherently generous and kind.

Avery considered their question. "Well, we'd bake cookies and take them to our neighbors. Then there was the sleigh ride through the park —it was always lit up with lights and decorations and such. And then, of course, we'd build a snowman."

Emmilia grabbed Avery's hand. "Let's do all of them."

"Yes!" Carlotta agreed as she grabbed Avery's other hand.

Matteo started. His sisters were trained not to touch people. It was a royal rule. One did not hang on a person. And yet, they'd taken to Avery as if she were one of the family.

Avery didn't seem to mind. She smiled at both girls. "I would like that very much. But I don't want to impose."

"Who's imposing?" asked Padre as he strode into the room, Madre on his arm. They made quite the striking couple with Madre's stunning good looks and Padre's kingly countenance, even in their silly cream sweaters with nutcrackers on the front. Padre must truly love

Madre if he was willing to pull that thing over his head.

Matteo stepped slightly in front of Avery, wanting to keep her out from under his father's critical eye.

"No one is imposing," Emmilia giggled at him. She wasn't cowed by Padre's sternness. "We're going to bake cookies with Avery tomorrow."

"And then take them to our neighbors," added Carlotta. Her smile tripped into a confused look. "Who are our neighbors?"

Padre and Madre exchanged a look that said they weren't too happy with the idea of their daughters showing up unannounced on a doorstep in the village below.

Avery patted their backs. "A neighbor is someone who lives close to you."

"Like *Bambinaia.* She helps take care of us," Emmilia announced proudly.

"And *il cuoco,* the cook—he makes wonderful sandwiches," Carlotta added.

Avery nodded. "I'm sure they'd love cookies from you two. It's not really about the cookies, although they are delicious; it's about sharing. And you two sound like you know how to share."

Before Madre or Padre could comment or ask for an introduction, Angelo and his wife,

Aria, joined them. Aria's sweater matched Angelo's. It barely stretched over her baby bump. Her pregnancy would be announced at the ball—the whole country would rejoice that the monarchy continued. Angelo was looking at his phone as he walked, his face drawn. "Our photographer can't make it through the storm. He's not coming," he said flatly.

Madre gasped. "But this is the only time we have to take this picture. If he doesn't come tonight, it will not be done. What will we do?"

"I'll take your picture," offered Avery, ducking out from behind Matteo.

Everyone turned to stare at her.

To her credit, she didn't shrink under the incredulous eyes of a king, a queen, and the princes and princesses of Isola. She smiled and pulled out her phone, which she wiggled for emphasis. "It's got a great camera."

Matteo wilted inside for her. She had no idea she was standing with the royal family. Granted, they didn't look royal in their crazy Christmas sweaters. They looked like a normal family. She was already under the impression he was a butler; perhaps she assumed his father was too. He had to fight his smile at the thought of Padre being mistaken for a butler. It made him seem more human in a way.

However, he was the king. These photos were for the family album, and neither Padre nor Madre would allow a stranger to take the photos.

As wonderful as Avery was with his sisters, she was going to be dismissed by Padre. And then he might never see her again. Which would truly be a shame, because he was beginning to grow fond of this American who had landed on his doorstep in a snowstorm.

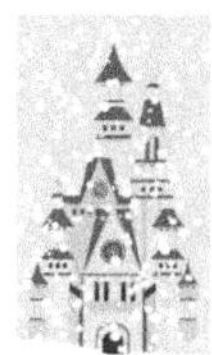

All eyes turned on her with a level of focus she hadn't experienced before. It was unnerving. But she continued to smile. She had, after all, stumbled right in the middle of their family moment.

If she could help them get their picture, then it wouldn't seem so weird, right? And maybe they'd excuse her for wandering the castle once again. Honestly, she was trying to find an exit. Why didn't they label doors in this country?!

Matteo's dad turned to his mom to decide if Avery could snap a picture or two. Matteo's parents looked a lot alike—one of those brother/sister couples. They had the same color hair as Matteo. Well, everyone in the family had the same hair, she realized as she looked around. They all had the same deep green eyes too, though Matteo's were much warmer than the others. His sister-in-law had darker hair and was lighter in coloring—like Snow White. She stood out but was just as beautiful. The whole family was beautiful.

So unfair.

"This is our private holiday portrait," said the mom.

Avery nodded. "What if I send the pictures to you right after I take them and then delete the images from my phone?" It would be a shame. She'd love to have a picture of Matteo to take home with her. No one would believe that a family of butlers was this good-looking. It must be the fact that they live in the castle. Was it possible to be ugly when you grew up in a fairy tale?

Matteo cleared his throat. "Madre, let her take the photos. I will make sure she keeps her word."

His mom softened. "Thank you." She turned to Avery. "And thank you for offering your services to our family. We are humbled."

Avery's mouth hung open. Humbled? Dang,

these had better be some good pictures. "I'll do my best." She stepped back and looked at all of them. "Do you have a regular pose, or would you like me to position you?" She'd done well on the trip, getting larger group pictures. This was no different. Okay, it was hugely different, because it mattered a whole lot more and she'd only have a few minutes to get it right.

"Whatever is *veloce*," said his dad. He had the bearing of a man who didn't like to stand around and wasn't often asked to do so.

"Of course." Avery went to work, showing them where to stand. She had a mom and dad in the middle, his hand on her back. The two girls stood in front of them, slightly facing one another. Finally, Matteo's married brother and his wife were next to the dad and Matteo next to his mom. "I like the sweaters," she said. "They're cute."

His mom beamed. "I thought they were whimsical."

"You picked them out?" Avery asked, even though the answer was obvious.

"Yes. We are a typical family at Christmas, *si?*"

Avery stifled her giggle. These people were anything but typical. They were formal and regal and beautiful beyond any of the holiday cards her family ever sent out; those cards had been wonderful but average. She wasn't going to burst her bubble. "*Si*," she replied.

They all beamed as if they'd accomplished something phenomenal, and she snapped the last picture. "I think that's it."

The family broke up with some hurried goodbyes. Mom motioned for the girls to get going. "Don't forget," Emmilia said over her shoulder. "Cookies tomorrow night at seven. Meet us here."

"You can count on it." Avery waved at them. In no time, it was just her and Matteo. She suddenly felt shy and underdressed in her jeans and flannel shirt. She tucked her hands in her pockets. "You have a great family. Dad's a bit stiff, but I think he might have cracked a smile there at the end."

Matteo laughed, placing his hand on his belly. "Come. You can download the images to a computer in the greeting room." He motioned for her to proceed him. She stepped to the side, choosing to walk with him since she had no idea where she was going.

"I don't know that I've ever been in a greeting room before."

His forehead wrinkled. "What room do you sit for tea with guests?"

"The kitchen."

He shook his head. "That wouldn't do. There's too much activity and too many listening ears."

"Maybe in *your* kitchen." Their meals were brought down from the kitchens, and she doubted Matteo's family had a cooking space of their own.

They entered the greeting room through a wide doorway and came into a space that could only be described as friendly. The furniture was arranged so that several small conversations or one large one could take place. The walls were cream with the dark molding that ran throughout the castle and bespoke of money in the coffers. The carpet was soft under her shoes. Honey-colored, it blended well with the tan accents. But it was the artwork that drew her eye. Done in bolds, the countryside and seaside paintings breathed life into the space.

"Here." Matteo motioned to a computer on a side table. "There are cords in the drawer. One of them should fit your phone."

She got down to business, finding the right attachment and uploading the images. "So …" She glanced up from where the bar on the screen slowly filled with color, indicating that the pictures were loading—ever so slowly. For a modern country, the computer was ancient. Matteo looked up from where he glanced through a ski magazine. "It's great that your whole family can live here and work here. What is it that you do?"

He shut the magazine. "I'm an advisor of sorts. Most days, I think they only keep me around because my dad is so important."

"That must be nice." The bar filled and a thumbs-up appeared, indicating that she was done. She pulled the cord and began highlighting the images on her phone so she could delete them. Such. A. Shame. But she'd given her word to his mom and didn't dare try to keep one.

"Why would you say that?" he asked.

She looked up from her task to find him looking at her with that intensity that she now knew was a family trait. Coming from him, it felt like the look penetrated her heart.

Perhaps it was the depth in which his eyes bored into hers, or maybe the sense that he truly wanted to know her, that made her share the truth. "I don't have family, so no one keeps me around."

His face softened. "My sisters may never let

you go. It was a dirty trick promising them cookies."

She laughed. "I could deal with that." She turned her phone around so he could see the screen. "Here's the images. I'm deleting them." She pressed the garbage can, and they began to disappear.

He reached for her phone, his fingers gliding over hers and sending sugar-flavored shivers over her skin. He scrolled through her pictures. "You visited the Vatican? Did you enjoy your time there?"

Immediately remembering some of the embarrassing pictures she'd taken, copying faces in paintings and poses of statues, she held out her hand. "I did. It was strange to see paintings from my history books in real life."

He handed over the phone.

A man in a suit arrived in the doorway and clicked his wooden-heeled shoes together to announce himself. "*Signore,* your evening appointment awaits."

"I'll be right there, Alfredo." Matteo took her hand and pulled her to her feet. His thumb brushed across her knuckles, and her knees went weak. Who knew she had a thing for butlers—er, advisors? "I will see you tomorrow for cookies?"

He pulled her left hand to his mouth and kissed her fingers.

She mumbled the world's most intelligent response. "Uh-huh."

"I look forward to it." He slipped his hand across hers as he left.

She melted into the couch and sighed.

Alfredo cleared his throat. The noise was startlingly loud and disapproving. Avery leapt to her feet. "*Signorina,* this way to the servants' quarters." He held out a white-gloved hand, indicating that she should start walking.

With a last look around the greeting room, she beamed. It really was a beautiful room. "Alfredo?"

"*Si, signorina?*" His gravelly voice was *high in the instep,* as her dad would have said.

"Can I get a picture with you?"

"With me, *signorina?*" The wrinkles around his eyes seemed to iron out with surprise.

She bit her lip. "You look—" She waved her hand in front of him. "—official."

He puffed out his chest. "I strive for *ufficiale.*"

She grinned and stepped so that they were both in the frame. Her smile was a contrast to Alfredo's determined aloofness. His green vest and silver-and-green-striped tie screamed Isola de la Familia. She could probably use his shirt collar as a cutting board, it was so stiff.

She hit the button and the phone made a clicking noise. "Thanks."

"My pleasure." He inclined his head and then once again motioned for her to proceed him down that hallway.

"Why do you do that? I don't know which way to go."

He paused for a moment. "A lady always knows where she's going."

She smirked. "I ain't no lady." But she started off, counting on him to stop her if she went the wrong way.

He sniffed. "I believe you could be."

His quiet, confident statement gave her pause. "I used to know what I wanted and where I was headed. But then, the world shifted on me. The rules changed."

"In that case, may I suggest figuring out where you are, and then deciding where you want to be?" He opened a door.

She looked in, down the hallway, and saw the servants' Christmas tree. "I guess I will know where this door leads, from now on."

"It is a start, *signorina*."

He shut the door behind her, and she turned,

filling her lungs with air. "A lady always knows where she's going …" She shook her head but stopped. "Figure out where I am …"

She headed to the Christmas tree and sat down cross-legged in front of it. The white lights gleamed, reflecting off the multicolored ornaments. The tree itself smelled like pine. A real tree, just like home. She reached out and felt the prickly needles. They bent easily under her touch. "Someone cares about you," she said, noting the water level in the tree stand.

"Where am I?" she asked out loud. She'd never thought about how much she used her parents as a reference point for herself until they were gone. Nine months was a long time, and yet it seemed like yesterday. And yet, it seemed like forever ago too. It was like that one event had become her starting and ending point in history.

But she didn't want it to stay that way. There were so many other wonderful moments she'd shared with her parents that deserved a higher place on the tree, as it were.

She may have been lost before, but in this moment, she knew right where she was. Remembering her parents and the Christmases they'd shared was a place of joy. That was where she decided to stay—to live.

"Thanks, Alfredo." She brushed the tree one more time and then set out to find Brandy. They needed some serious chocolate and girl talk. It was time to chat about the advisor and his deep green eyes.

CHAPTER 8

MATTEO

Matteo shifted, uncomfortable under Luciana's falsely adoring gaze. The woman hadn't stopped staring at him long enough to finish her *primi* before the soup was whisked away and replaced with a main dish.

The castle had many places to host a meal—er, date. He still had a hard time thinking of this as a date. Probably because the arrangements were made by his steward and her assistant. Perhaps the two of them should get together and see if there were sparks between them, because there weren't any between Matteo and Luciana.

What was between them? Cooked fish.

"Do you like your fish breaded or grilled?" he asked, nodding his head at her untouched plate.

She jerked in surprise, knocking a fork onto the floor, which she ignored. As did he. "I adore all fish that's caught off our coasts." She blinked slowly. Wait, was she trying to wink at him? Over fish?

He steeled himself. It wasn't that Luciana wasn't a nice person; it was just that he'd never been able to get more than a surface answer out of her. Perhaps if he tried a deeper subject, they might be able to make some headway.

He placed his arm on the table and leaned over, hoping to add weight to his question. "Luciana, we have never … talked about the expectations before us."

Her eyes dropped to her plate, and she slid her spoon into alignment with the rest of the silverware.

"What are your expectations for us?" he prompted. If he had to drag answers out of her, this would be a long evening indeed.

"That we marry as our families have long spoken of."

That was a stretch. His madre had made a veiled comment to her madre over a decade ago that they might suit well, and from then on, he'd been hooked by her net. "Yes, but what about after that? What do you want in a *marito*, a husband?"

She brought her eyes up to meet his. "I want a prince."

He fell back in his seat. "Is that all? Just by being born with a title, I will have met all your expectations?"

She nodded, her expression clear and honest.

Well, that was disappointing. He'd hoped for a challenge of some sort, something he could aspire to in the coming years. "What of a family? *Bambini?*"

"Oh, well. I am open to having one child. It will make a good showing to the public. But any more than that and I'll ruin my figure. A princess has to remain thin her whole life long, and I'm up for the challenge of keeping myself in physical shape."

He closed his fist under the table. A princess should be so much more than physically fit. She should be kind, charitable, graceful, and knowledgeable about politics and economics.

And a wife? His wife? He had so many more qualities he wanted. The first among them was that the woman loved him. *Him.* Not his crown. The second was that she wanted children. Those were his two deal-breaker requirements.

"I'd always seen myself as the father of three."
He didn't know where the number came from
initially, but it had been the idea that followed
him whenever he thought about being a padre.

"Isn't that excessive for the second son? I
mean, it's not like you have to worry about
continuing the blood line. Angelo will take care
of that." She flicked a piece of shiny hair off her
cheek, and it settled in just the right spot to frame
her face. She had grace and beauty, he couldn't
deny that, but she lacked in the areas that meant
more to him.

It also raked across his back that she'd
compared him to his brother. Everyone did it, so
he shouldn't have been surprised. But he thought
his future wife should see *him* alone and not in
the shadow of his older brother. The man he was
and the man he wanted to be—a woman who
could see those things was a jewel to be treasured.

"I wouldn't have children out of obligation,
Luciana. I would have them because I want to be
a padre, to have a family of my own."

She balked. "You can't be serious."

"Do you not want to be a mother?"

"No. I mean, I'll bear a child—it is my duty to
the country—but I have no desire to change
messy *pannolini* like a *bambinaia*."

Well, at least she had some spunk in her. Matteo motioned discreetly for their plates to be taken. He'd lost his appetite, and she hadn't touched a morsel. The server arrived, wearing the traditional white shirt and deep green vest. He scooped up their plates. Right behind him was another man with dessert.

"Are you going to eat that?" Matteo asked.

Luciana sighed wearily. "I'd better not. The ball is in four days, and I have to fit into my dress."

"You look like you could fit into one of my pant legs."

She giggled. "I think that's the nicest thing you've ever said to me."

He sighed. It was probably true. "Luciana, I must apologize for not being kinder to you over the years. I will be honest—I do not do well being told what to do. But you did not deserve to be ignored. I am afraid that we have missed out on what could have been a solid ..." Not friendship— goodness, no. They did not see things the same way. She saw them much as his padre did, and Matteo did not appreciate his vision. "... acquaintance."

Her teeth nearly blinded him when she

smiled. "No need to apologize. We will have many years to become acquainted."

He didn't comment. Instead, he stood and offered her his hand to get up. She took it, and he had to stifle another sigh. No sparks. No tingles. No increase in heart rate. He kissed the back of her hand in farewell, and she lifted her skirts and made her way out of the room.

Matteo hung back. When she was gone, he sat down at the table and dug into his *tartufo*. The chocolate shell broke easily and revealed the vanilla gelato inside. He dug deeper, going for the strawberry center.

Alfredo stepped into the room and stood at attention just inside the doorway.

Matteo, his mouth full, motioned for him to come over. "Sit, Alfredo."

Alfredo looked down at the recently vacated chair as if it were a snake about to bite him. "*Signore*, I would never presume to join you at the table."

"Then stop presuming and sit down. I have a question to ask, and I can't do it with you hovering." He was on the breakthrough of a decision; couldn't the man see that?

Alfredo pulled the chair out and sat on the edge of it. "Very well. I've sat."

"Eat." Matteo pointed to the dessert. "You might as well. It will go to waste."

Alfredo used his gloved hand to push the plate slightly farther away from him. "Your question?"

"I assume you were listening in on my recent conversation?" It was a reasonable assumption. His steward was almost always within calling distance. And he had ears like an owl—Matteo rarely had to raise his voice to find Alfredo. He took another delicious bite of gelato. For some reason, he felt free and reckless. Perhaps because he'd come to understand something that he'd only hoped was true before.

"*Si, signore.*"

"Good. Then you'll understand when I tell you that I will not marry Luciana. She is not the woman for me, and I will cause a civil war before I will tie myself to her until death do us part."

"I believe your discernment and decision in this area is well founded. If there is to be a coup, the gelato will not be missed." Alfredo deliberately picked up the dessert spoon, broke the chocolate shell, and took a small amount of gelato.

Shocked at the breach in protocol, it took Matteo a moment to respond. "Thank you."

They sat for several spoonfuls of silence.

"Perhaps there is another option for a bride, *signore*," Alfredo ventured.

Matteo rubbed his jaw with his thumb. "You could be right. What do you think of the American?" Alfredo had escorted Avery back to the servants' quarters. Matteo was beginning to wonder how she kept getting out into the castle. Was she prone to wandering? Did she get lost often? Every question he had about her only raised five more.

For example, what did she mean when she said she didn't have family? Was it possible that she was all alone in the world? If so, he wanted to help her, to give her a place to belong—in his heart, if possible. Though they didn't know one another well enough to hope for such a thing.

"I think she's bold and presumptuous," Alfred replied.

Matteo grinned. "*Si.*"

"And she has a good heart, much like a *principe* who used to give his sisters piggyback rides through the hallways."

Matteo smiled at the memory. He wondered if his sisters would appreciate the offer now; they'd already grown so much. He owed them, though. It was because of them that he had a date to make cookies tomorrow night. He couldn't wait to spend time with Avery, to find the answers to his questions. Perhaps he would learn that they, too, did not suit. He doubted it, though. Every part of him wanted every part of her.

It wasn't a coincidence that she was here at this time in his life. Of that, he was certain. But what role she would play in his future? That was yet to be determined.

CHAPTER 9

AVERY

"Will you stop looking around like that?"

"Ow." Avery pulled her arm back to glare at Brandy, who'd just smacked her. "I'm supposed to look around; it's a palace tour."

"You're looking for your mystery man and completely missing the Baroque paintings and architecture that give this place its charm." She wrinkled her nose as if saying all that was difficult.

Avery laughed. "You sound more like Sabrina every day. You could apply for a job in the castle." Sabrina was beyond thrilled that she'd gotten approval to give them the standard tour of the castle even though it was closed for the holidays. Apparently, living there had its privileges. In truth, they'd all snuck out at one time or another to explore. Greg insisted that as long as they looked like they knew where they were going, no one would stop them.

If Sabrina knew they were traipsing about, she'd pitch a fit and lock them in the dungeon.

So far, only Avery had been caught—and that hadn't turned out too bad, considering she was invited back for Christmas cookies.

Her heart skipped a beat as she thought about Matteo and the way he treated his little sisters. Swoon! Any guy who took time for his family was at the top of her good list.

On top of all the giddy feelings coursing through her over Matteo, she had a craving for sugar cookies that couldn't go unanswered for much longer or she'd turn into a Grinch.

Up front, Sabrina went on about a painting that was over 1200 years old. The person's name was unknown, but the image, a naked man with a bow and arrow, was regarded as one of the best paintings from its period and had been in the royal family's possession since the castle was built. Avery averted her eyes as they walked by.

They'd seen plenty of such artwork on their tour, and small-town girl that she was, it still embarrassed her.

Brandy reached out to run her hand along the wainscoting. There were small bees carved into it, making their way lazily around the hallway. "Maybe you should apply for a job here. Then you and your advisor man could raise children in these halls where they're probably not allowed to touch anything."

Avery frowned, thinking of the extremely well-behaved girls she'd met the day before. They were children. They should have been romping around, playing tag or something. Instead, they stood still with better posture than she'd ever had —as an adult or a child. Their sweet smiles were full of the joy that children who hadn't seen bad things in the world held in their hearts. She used to be one of those kids. Was one too long, perhaps. Because when something truly horrible did happen, she was unprepared to face it.

"My children will have messy fingers and dirty faces as often as we can manage it," Avery vowed. And so would those girls by the time she was done with them tonight. "If there's one thing I've learned, it's that you have to seize the opportunities for good times when they come, even if it means cleaning up a mess."

"Hear, hear." Brandy side-hugged her. "You seem to be coming to a lot of realizations about life lately. What's up with that?"

Avery grew shy. She'd told Brandy about Matteo, but she'd left out the conversation with Alfredo where he'd encouraged her to get her head on straight. It was kind of embarrassing that he'd pegged her so easily. Not that he knew her history, but that was what made his observations all the more honest and hard to dismiss. If he'd known what she'd been through, he might have taken pity on her and not said a word. That would have been worse. Because what he did say, that she had potential, had spurred her to strive for it.

She gathered her thoughts before saying, "I think … well, I feel like some of the fog is clearing and I'm figuring out who I am now. I'm different than I was before—but I'm also the same."

Brandy grinned. "Still have a soft spot for gelato?"

Avery laughed. "I don't think anything could cure that." They moved into the ballroom, where workers hung garlands and decorated trees in preparation for the Christmas Eve ball. The room was a mess that would soon be magical—the anticipation in the air was enough to spin circles on.

"The royal family has hosted a Christmas Eve ball consecutively since the castle was built in the 13th century. In the beginning, it was a small family affair that grew to include dignitaries from all over Europe." Sabrina pointed at the floor. "The floor has been replaced three times. The original was marble. During World War I …"

"So what's the biggest thing you've concluded about yourself?" asked Brandy. She tipped her head back to look at the gold filigree on the ceiling.

Avery paused and searched her thoughts. "That I'm a creature made of love. I can't hold it back, and I can't live without it. It's time for me to start sharing that again."

Brandy squeezed her arm.

Avery smiled to herself as she followed the group into the formal dining room with its impossibly long table and stunning holly centerpieces. Maybe she could share a piece of her heart with Matteo. It wasn't put back together, but what was there worked.

And she couldn't think of a guy she'd rather test it out on than him. His kindness to his sisters, his deep and probing gazes, and his quiet humor made her think that he wasn't the kind of man to take such a gift lightly. She only hoped that when the time came, she didn't chicken out.

CHAPTER 10

AVERY

Avery was more than a little disappointed when the only people waiting for her in the entrance hall were two excited girls and their nanny. She'd conjured up all sorts of scenarios that always seemed to end with her in Matteo's arms and soft kisses in the sunshine, moonlight, and falling snow. She'd spent a lot of time thinking about him. Which was unusual, because she hadn't thought about much for a while—just drifting where life took her.

She was ready to be proactive.

Activity tonight meant making a special memory for two Isoladian children who had never baked cookies before. She hugged them both hello. At first their arms were stiff and their backs straight, but she wiggled side to side and infused as much love into the hug as possible, testing out her theory that she was a creature made to love. They soon relaxed and hugged her fully.

Then she hugged the nanny, Mia.

"Oof!" Mia patted Avery's back. "*Gratzie?*"

The girls giggled. Avery guessed the nanny didn't get hugged that often. All the more reason she should have one now.

They made their way to the kitchen, a big, beautiful room with a solid granite countertop that went on for miles. At the far side of the room, several cooks kneaded bread by hand. They had rolling carts of dough waiting and others partially filled to proof overnight. Avery looked closer and found physical traits that told her they were related. She grinned. The family business of bread making in the castle was one she wouldn't mind adopting into.

Avery ran her hand over the countertop. It was smooth and cool to the touch and sparkling clean. She glanced at the small doorways on either end of the kitchen. "I can't imagine what it took to get this in here."

Mia smiled. "I believe they built the castle around it."

"Really?" Avery asked, stunned that such a thing would enter the designers' minds that long ago.

The girls laughed. "She's teasing you," Carlotta pointed out. "But that means she likes you, so don't be offended." She looked at her nanny with affection.

"Is that how it is around here?" she asked, thinking of the times Matteo had teased her.

The three of them nodded, making her feel as though she'd been inducted into an exclusive club.

"Then it's game on." She rubbed her palms together.

A sous chef appeared. "*Permesso*, your ingredients." He half bowed and waved to a counter near the ovens, where containers of all sizes waited for them. He stepped to the nearest oven and placed his hand over the control. "What temperature would you like, *signorina?*"

"Three hundred and fifty," she answered as she accepted the white apron he offered her.

His mind ticked as he did the calculations from Fahrenheit, and then set he the oven. The girls had matching ones, though they had to make knots in the neck loop so they stayed up high enough to protect their clothing.

And what beautiful clothing it was. Designer pants and sweaters—they dressed like a clothing ad. Avery glanced down at her plaid shirt layered over a matching tee shirt. She'd packed layers for the trip, not castle attire. No one else seemed to notice that one of these things was not like the others, so she decided not to worry over it. This was one of those *grab the joy while you can* moments.

Avery grabbed the butter and eyeballed a cup, ignoring the scale and earning her a stunned look from the sous chef. He shook his head and made himself scarce, probably worried that her shoddy baking skills would rub off on him. Little did he know, Mom's cookies were foolproof.

"Don't we need a recipe?" Emmilia's little forehead creased with worry. "What if we make a mistake?"

Avery caught a little more than just a child's worry about cookies in there. The girls acted so grown up for their age. Perhaps they had perfectionist tendencies. "I have the recipe memorized. And if we mess up, we'll start over and try again."

"Will we have time?" Carlotta checked her phone and then tucked it back in her pocket.

Avery was surprised to see such a young girl

have a phone, but again, they acted years older than their age. "We'll make time," Avery assured them.

"But we have dance lessons at eight-thirty." Emmilia was working herself up into a tizzy.

"How about we don't worry about it until it becomes a problem? No sense borrowing stress, as my mom used to say." She smiled, grateful for her mother's words of wisdom; she'd probably had fifteen sayings that she'd cycled through as Avery had grown up. She should write them down. No, she *would* write them down—tonight. She had a travel journal she could use. It would be a good way to remember her mother, and it would be a nice memorial so she didn't forget when she had girls of her own to nurture through the terrible thirteens.

Emmilia nodded, and Avery gave her a side hug of assurance.

Mia smiled at her. "You're good with children, *si?*"

It had taken Avery a bit to get used to the fact that Isoladians weren't really asking questions when they ended a sentence with *si?* Sabrina had explained that it was like an American saying *right?* at the end of a sentence. She glanced at the door, wondering if Matteo had forgotten about their evening. He'd seemed interested, though not quite eager. Maybe she'd read too much into his polite conversation.

"Thanks. I've always wanted to be a mom." As she talked, she showed the girls how to scoop sugar and then spoon baking powder and salt into the mix.

"That's a fine aspiration." Mia counted out eggs, demonstrating how to break them on a flat surface. The girls followed along, squealing when the yolk dripped out.

"What about you?" Avery asked her in return.

"I will be with these girls until they are eighteen." She smiled fondly at them. "At that time, I will see what else there is to do with my life."

"I'm so impressed with the dedication everyone has to their occupations—planning families around them and such. In America, it's the other way around: we plan work around our families—well, if we can." She didn't want to put down the way of life here, but the obsession with work and obligation was overwhelming. Matteo and the girls lived in the palace because their dad was an advisor. The position must be really important to the king to allow them to live there, and it probably made balancing a family and career easier. But it just seemed like a lot to ask of a family man.

"We believe everyone has a purpose in life. Some people are born into theirs, while others have to search. Being born into a position is a privilege; it means you know who you are. Others feel like finding their way is what they want."

They'd added the eggs and were almost ready to add the flour. She had the mixer going, wanting to make sure the vanilla was worked into the batter. Emmilia dumped flour in, and the whole thing puffed up into the air and settled on them, on the counter, and on the floor.

Avery stood with her arms in front of her, her mind blank with shock.

"Oh no!" The poor girl gasped, and tears filled her eyes. "I didn't mean to. I'm so sorry."

Avery looked at each of them. Snow dusted their hair, their cheeks, and their clothing. She burst out laughing. "We look like snowmen."

Emmilia sniffled a couple times before she dared smile. "Snow women."

Taking a pinch of flour, Avery tossed it at Emmilia. "You missed a spot."

Emmilia blinked several times, her mouth open in shock. "You threw flour."

"Yes." Avery did the same at Carlotta, who dodged, laughing. "It's just flour."

The girls giggled. "I fear Madre would not approve." Carlotta patted her hair, and a puff of flour came out.

"I fear you are *corretto*."

They all spun to find Matteo leaning against the doorway, his arms bulging against his button-up shirt and his hair perfectly mussed. Even at the end of a day, he looked yummy.

Avery pressed her lips together and grabbed a dish towel to wipe off her face. "We were just baking."

Matteo strode in, confident, strong, and so darn manly it was a sin. "I thought you were having a food fight, *si*?" He pinched the flour and sprinkled it over Avery's head.

She blew at it, making it cloud in his face. The girls laughed, and Mia turned away to hide her snicker.

"You are a bad influence on my sisters." He took the towel from her and wiped his face.

The girls switched from giggles to frowns so quickly it was alarming. Avery hurried to rescue them and bring back some of the happiness they'd shared before. "I suppose I am—if this were naughty. But no one got on Santa's naughty list for spilling flour—trust me." She winked at the girls, and they both relaxed. "Anyway, spills can be cleaned, but memories last forever."

Matteo began rolling up his sleeves. "Very well. What should I do?"

"You are going to bake?" Carlotta put her hand on her hip.

"Yes. And I plan to help with deliveries too."

Avery stared at him. A man who was important enough to wear a business suit all day and into the kitchen at night—and look darn good doing it—shouldn't be smiling at her like that. Like he wanted to spend time with her and there was nowhere else he'd dream of going. She bit her lip. "I thought you'd forgotten about this." She made a small circle with her hand, including herself in there. Because she'd feared he'd forgotten about her, too.

Matteo captured her eyes with his. "Never."

"Who would you take them to?" asked Emmilia, completely unaware of the temperature ticking up, up, up until Avery thought she might burst. If Matteo looked at her like that again, she'd be able to cook the dough without the oven.

"Alfredo," Matteo announced.

Carlotta giggled. "I don't think he likes sweets. He's grouchy."

Matteo winked at Avery, awakening the butterflies in her stomach. "I have it on good authority that he enjoys them—immensely."

They all set to work, hurrying to accomplish their task before the girls' dance lesson. Matteo turned on two more ovens and dug out another bowl for frosting. With several ovens going at once, the cookies baked in record time. They were transferred to the cooling racks in the pantry while the crew made and sampled vanilla icing.

"I am beginning to see the benefits of baking." Matteo swiped a spoon through the frosting and put it in his mouth. "Hmm—dis id *delizioso*."

Avery wasn't the only girl to giggle.

Emmilia took it up on herself to reprimand her older brother for his manners. "We do not speak with our mouths full." She took a bite of a cookie.

He reached over and tickled her. "What about laugh? Can we laugh with our mouths full?"

She shook her head. Her face turned red with the effort it took to hold her mouth closed while she laughed.

Matteo kissed her cheek and released her. "You are far too grown-up."

"I agree." Carlotta lifted a prim nose at them

all. "Which is why I think we should build snowmen tomorrow morning."

Mia pulled out her phone and tapped on the calendar app. "We have an opening at ten." She looked at Avery. "Will that work for you?"

Avery chuckled. "I'll have to check with my secretary, but I'm pretty sure I'm open."

Matteo mock-frowned. "Am I not invited?"

The ladies exchanged looks asking each other who was going to give him the bad news.

He pouted. "I will bring the coins for eyes and buttons if you pleeease let me come."

"What do you think, girls?" Avery asked while swiping frosting on the last cookie.

He reached over and took a bite of it while it was still in her hand. Moaning with pleasure, he collapsed against the counter. "Never mind, I'll stay here and eat cookies. You can go."

She swatted at his chest, thoroughly enjoying this side of him that hammed it up for his sisters. "We're giving these away." She glanced down at the one now missing a bite. "Except this one. You can have it." She handed it to him.

He stood and broke a corner off. "You have to taste it."

She gave him a disbelieving look.

"What if it's horrible and I feed it to Alfredo and he dies?"

She shook out her apron. "Don't even joke about that." With a quick move, she bit the piece of cookie right out of his hand. The brief contact sent better-than-frosting shivers over her skin. The world slowed down and shrank until it was just the two of them, staring into one another's eyes and trying to breathe. The taste of cream cheese frosting on her tongue built her desire to see if he tasted just as good.

His eyes dipped to her lips.

Mia started chatting loudly with the girls, moving about quickly as she tidied up. "Well, look at that—we need to hurry if we'll be ready for dance lessons."

"Oh!" Avery started, coming back to the moment. "Take this plate—it's for their teacher. And this one is for you."

Mia grinned and dipped a curtsy. *"Gratzie, mi amica."*

"What about the rest?" asked Carlotta, surveying the full plates on the counter.

Matteo bowed. "If you will trust your older brother, I promise you each plate of cookies will find a home before the night is through."

Carlotta nodded at him. "*Bueno*—but no eating them!" She pointed her finger at his nose.

He nodded solemnly.

Avery's heart warmed at the scene, and she let out a gusty sigh. Realizing how loud the sound was, she turned away to rinse out a dishcloth. The girls stopped to hug her, easily this time, and say their goodbyes.

In moments, she was alone with Matteo. All day, she'd been thinking about being with him again. Now that she had him to herself, she wasn't sure what to do with him.

"I think that's everyone on the list." Matteo tucked his phone back in his pocket and frowned at the two remaining plates in Avery's hands. "Did you make too many cookies?" He chastened himself for sounding so critical. When did he become a grump? Delivering cookies to the staff had been a surprise joy—one he hadn't known could happen.

And one he should have saved for his sisters to at least sample. They would have thrilled to see the light on the dress maker's face. Matilda had sewn gowns for the girls since their christenings and loved them so much. When Matteo told her the girls baked the cookies for her, she acted as though an angel had stirred the batter. Then she kissed him on both cheeks.

Avery laughed at his accusation. "Okay, first of all, there's no such thing as too many cookies."

He grinned—and not for the first time that night. Avery had a way with people. She just … loved them right away. It was the strangest thing he'd ever seen. There was no waiting on pretense or walls to break through. Just a sense that she was put here to spread happiness.

It spread to him as easily as frosting on a cookie.

"Second of all, this one is for Alfredo." She held one plate out to him. "Because you said you wanted to give him a plate, *si?*"

"Who's the other one for?" He lifted his chin to keep an eye on it as she turned her body slightly, shielding her treasure.

"You'll find out when the time comes."

He shrugged, perfectly happy to follow her around for a couple more hours if need be. He checked his phone. "I believe Alfredo is in the greenhouse this time of night." He held out his arm for her to take. "*Lo facciamo?*"

She smiled shyly as she slipped her hand into the crook of his arm. "We shall."

He liked that she wasn't grabby. He'd dated

many women who pawed him like eager kittens looking for a treat. While it was flattering that they saw him as something yummy, he didn't appreciate being manhandled. Avery was shy, and that was foreign in his world.

They made it through the castle and crossed the ten feet from the atrium to the greenhouse. Stepping inside was like walking into a tropical paradise. Flowers, fruit and palm trees, and plants of every kind were arrayed in their leafy green state. The air was moist and warm, immediately chasing the cold off their skin and clothes.

Avery groaned. "There goes my hair." She reached up and pressed her palms to her head.

"What do you mean?" He looked her over to see if anything was amiss, but she seemed just as perfect as she had when sprinkling flour on his sister's head.

"The humidity. My curls will go nuts." She said this with only a hint of regret—like it was something that couldn't be helped.

"Curly hair is a bad thing?" He looked up as if trying to see his own hair, which had a natural wave.

She gave his arm a squeeze. "Not really. But I worked hard for this look, and I wanted it to stay straight."

He felt something warm grow in his chest. "You made an effort, knowing you would see me tonight?"

Her cheeks colored. "If you must know, yes. It's not every day that I bake with a royal advisor, and I wanted to look presentable."

Her words caused a shiver of ice to go down his back. She truly believed him to be on staff. It wasn't an insult, but it was disturbing, because he didn't know if she would treat him differently if she knew he was a prince. In truth, she would *have* to treat him differently; there were protocols to follow. Somehow, the idea of her curtsying to him felt wrong. She was no ordinary woman. He traced a finger down her cheek. "You're prettier than the sunset over the sea."

Her face colored the same shade as the sunset, and he was thrilled that his words had brought out that beauty.

"*Signore?*" Alfredo's interruption couldn't have been more untimely. Then again, the man was known for his punctuality; perhaps some distance from the heady emotions and pounding in Matteo's chest was appropriate.

"Alfredo, we've come bearing gifts." Matteo presented the plate with all the flourish of a newly hired server out to impress.

Alfredo was not impressed with Matteo's theatrics. Not until his eyes landed on the bell-shaped goodies covered in sweet icing and sprinkles. "I'm sure these did not come from your efforts, *signore*." He turned to Avery and dipped his head in a bow. "The bounty must be from you, our American visitor."

Alfredo's accent on the word *visitor* sounded like a warning to Matteo—one he chose to ignore.

Avery's cheeks widened with her smile, and she bowed back to him. "I'm honored to share this dessert from my hometown to your table, *amico*. My mother's recipe never disappoints, and I hope you will enjoy every morsel." She glanced out of the corner of her eye at Matteo before adding. "But I can't take credit for delivery, because it was Matteo who wanted to make sure you were included in our holiday giving."

Alfredo turned to Matteo, his eyebrows raised.

Matteo burst out laughing. "Don't look so surprised. I couldn't forget you if I tried."

Alfredo nodded. "I suppose not." He lifted a cookie. "*Permesso?*"

"*Si, per favore*," Avery responded with a lilt.

"Your accent is quite remarkable," Matteo commented. "You almost sounded like one of us."

She lifted her shoulders and turned partway around and back, taking in the stunning flowers that grew in clumps around them. The glass was clean, but the snow piled up, leaving the greenhouse buried and quiet. "I could live here."

"Really?" It was Matteo's turn to raise his eyebrows in disbelief. "You would leave your country?"

She nodded and tucked some hair behind her ear. "I would. This place feels like it could be home, and I haven't felt that in a long time." She looked up to find both men considering her with warmth and compassion. As if feeling uncertain under the scrutiny, she giggled. "Don't looks so serious. Eat."

Alfredo followed her orders, but Matteo didn't have a cookie of his own, so he watched to see what his old friend, confidant, and in many ways mentor had to say. Alfredo closed his eyes and chewed slowly. "You are welcome to bring me cookies every day."

She laughed. "I'm not sure I'd be welcome in the kitchen—we made quite the mess."

"But she left the staff a dozen cookies as an

apology," Matteo was quick to add. He wanted Alfredo to like Avery—wanted it very much.

Alfredo took another, smaller bite this time. Then he said, "I'm sure they appreciated having someone cook for them for once."

Matteo tipped his head. "I hadn't thought of that."

Avery pointed to the last plate. "We should probably finish delivering."

"You are giving to others?" Alfredo asked, eyeing Matteo as if he were a fish flopping on the sand instead of swimming in the ocean.

Matteo's defenses rose. He was charitable. And yet … Avery was the one who hugged the nanny goodbye and thanked her. Avery was the one who left cookies for the cooks.

"We delivered eleven plates so far." Avery checked to make sure nothing had slipped on her plate. "This is the last one."

Alfredo turned to Matteo. "And you are helping?" he clarified.

Matteo shrugged. "*Si.*"

Alfredo looked at Avery once again. This time when he bowed, he moved from the waist. "You have done wonderful tonight, *amica.*"

Avery positively blossomed under his praise, though Matteo was the one who understood that

Alfredo was proud of her for getting him to think outside of himself.

Matteo was jealous that he hadn't been able to get the same response out of her when he'd called her beautiful. Then again, blushing like a schoolgirl was preferred to lighting up like a Christmas tree. The one meant her heart was learning a rhythm just for him. But the other … he wasn't sure why, but he wanted all her joys.

And her sorrows, if she would share them. She'd been happy tonight; the blanket of tragedy that followed her to Isola had thinned.

As they made their way back into the castle, Avery stopped and tipped her head back to catch a snowflake on her tongue. She stared up at the sky and took a deep breath. "Can you smell it?"

He sniffed quickly. "What?"

"Winter. It smells crisp and clean, cold and clear. There's no other smell like it in the world." She breathed again and then laughed. "Here, it comes with salt." She watched him. "Go on, try it. See if you can catch the scent."

Feeling silly doing this in front of her, Matteo gritted his jaw and took a deep breath, his nostrils flaring.

Avery laughed at him. Laughed! No one but his family dared to laugh at him. With him, yes.

But never at him. He deflated; at the same time, his pride swelled big enough to crowd out his good sense.

"You're doing it wrong." She flapped her free hand at him.

"I'm smelling wrong?" he growled back.

"Don't get your royal advisor undies twisted about it."

He blinked at the image her words painted and then wished he could get it out of his head.

"I'll show you." She put a hand on his shoulder. "Relax." She then moved it under his chin and tipped his face back so all he could see was the dark sky and snowflakes falling in no pattern or order. The image was positively tranquilizing.

Had he said he liked that she didn't touch him? Because now that her skin had made contact with his, he was abuzz with energy and desire. Her hands were warm and soft, and he wanted, more than anything, for her to slide them behind his head and bury them in his hair.

She dropped her fingers from his chin, and he immediately felt the loss. "Now …" Her voice was much softer, like she was having a hard time getting her words out. "Think of Christmas and presents and cider and pine trees and just breathe it all in."

He did as instructed, filling his chest and letting it expand beyond its normal efforts. His head spun, and he felt parts of him release that been held tight for years. With his eyes closed, he said, "You forgot the sugar, vanilla and cinnamon and …" He drew in another deep breath. "Honeysuckle."

He slowly opened his eyes and dropped his head so he could look at her, standing so close to him their breath puffed up in clouds, mingling together like dancers.

"Honeysuckle?" he asked.

"That's my perfume. I, uh, bought it in Florence."

He lifted one corner of his mouth. "It's *bella*. And it fits you."

"How so?" She cocked her head in the most adorable way. How could a woman be so sexy and so cute at the same time?

"It's sweet with undertones of sultry."

"Oh." Her mouth formed a small O, and it was all Matteo could do not to lean down and kiss her.

"You've ruined me, *mi fiore*."

She blinked rapidly. Matteo wondered how

good her Italian was—did she know he'd just called her *my flower*? Did he care if she figured it out? No. He did not. The nickname slipped out without planning or prep, and it matched how he felt when he looked at her. He saw beauty and grace and an acceptance of all around her. A flower didn't care if you were a prince or a steward or a butler or a cook. It just wanted to make the world better for being in it—like Avery.

He explained, "I shall never smell winter nor honeysuckle again and not think of you and this moment."

"Are we having a moment?" she asked quietly.

"I certainly hope so." Matteo took her hand.

She bit her lip and glanced down. "I don't—" She tried to pull away.

"*Per favore, me fiore*, allow me this. So that when I think upon this moment, I will know what it feels like to hold your hand in mine and believe that Christmas truly is a time of miracles."

"You think it would take a miracle for me to let you hold my hand?"

"I thought it would take more than that," he admitted.

She shook her head and tugged him toward the door. "Come on, before you feed me any more lines."

"I do not feed lines."

"You do. And you're excellent at it."

"This bothers you?" He wasn't quite sure what he'd done to have her brush away his affections like they were flour dust on her apron.

"Immensely." She nodded toward the door for Matteo to open it. He did, being the gentleman he was raised to be and not minding one bit.

He smiled as they made their way down the hall to the servants' door. "What is this?" Perhaps she wanted to gift cookies to her travel companions. Which was a wonderful idea, except that one of them was sure to recognize him as the prince, and then his time—his deeply fulfilling time with Avery as a man—would be over. He wasn't sure he was ready for that to happen, and so he stopped several feet from the doorway.

She glanced over her shoulder at him and then stopped and turned. "I'm going to call it a night. Thank you for making a wonderful memory for your sisters ... and for me."

"I will see you again, *si?*"

She nodded.

"*Bueno.*"

"Oh!" She handed over the plate of cookies. "These are for your brother and his wife."

Matteo balked. Certainly, she did not expect

him to take cookies to Angelo. The thought was absurd. They really weren't that close anymore. As children, they'd been the best of friends. He wasn't quite sure when they'd pulled away from one another, but the memories made him pine for easier times and less politics in their relationship. "Truly?"

"*Si.*"

"Why?"

She laughed and shoved his shoulder. "Because they're family."

"I thought cookies were for neighbors."

She smiled softly. "Family can be neighbors, and neighbors can be family. It's all in how you look at it." She leaned in and pressed a quick kiss to his cheek. The feel of her lips on his skin ignited a fire in his chest.

"Now who is bothering whom?" he whispered.

She winked.

She. Winked.

Matteo contemplated throwing the cookies over his shoulder and taking her in his arms when she slipped through the door and disappeared from sight.

"That woman," he mused. He hardly dared admit that she'd fully captured his attention—

even to himself. He'd rather continue on in a blissful state of denial that his actions—and his heart—were not behaving as a prince's should. He hated that a single kiss could mean the disruption of his entire country and hundreds of years of tradition.

Nevertheless, he was a prince and not ignorant of diplomacy. Perhaps with a bit of sugar applied to the gears, he'd be able to turn things his direction.

It was time to deliver cookies and gain an ally.

CHAPTER 12

MATTEO

Matteo knocked on the door to his brother's private suite and then stood back and waited. It took a moment for Luca, Angelo's steward, to answer the door.

"Ah, *Principe*." He stepped aside and motioned for Matteo to come in. "I shall tell the family you are here, *si*?" His eyes landed on the cookies, and interest blossomed. He wouldn't ask. And Matteo wasn't in the mood to explain how he'd been roped into participating in an American tradition by one beautiful woman and his two little sisters.

"*Gratzie*." Matteo held the plate out in front of him as he walked, keeping one eye on it and one eye on where he was going. As ridiculous as he felt at the moment, he would feel much worse if he had to tell Avery he'd dropped her cookies.

Angelo and Aria sat stiffly on the couch while Angelo tried to hold a lifelike baby doll. He was as awkward as a moose on ice skates. Aria's hands went out as if she were going to catch their practice bundle of joy, but she pulled them back.

"You have to hold her head," she admonished as the doll began to cry.

Matteo blinked at the sound.

"I'm trying." Angelo flopped the limp figure up to his shoulder, the face smacking his arm and making the doll cry louder. "Gah, here." He shoved the thing at Aria.

She shook her head at him fondly. "You can run a whole country, but you can't learn to hold a baby."

He stood up as if needing more distance between him and the doll. She stood as well, bouncing and rocking and cooing until the doll gurgled. Thank goodness one of them knew what they were doing.

Luca cleared his throat. "Principe Matteo has come for a visit, your highnesses." He bowed at the middle and then stepped smartly out of the room.

Angelo glared at him. "What are you doing

here?" No doubt he was embarrassed by his lack of parenting skills and snapping at Matteo because of it.

Matteo didn't often visit his brother unannounced. Now he knew why. "I brought you cookies."

Aria cupped the back of the doll's head and scooted towards him. "That was kind. What for?"

"Christmas." He smiled, offering the plate to her.

She took one and nibbled at it. "I shouldn't, but it's so good." She moaned. "I'm going to put this thing away. Hide those from me, will you?" she asked Angelo.

For the first time since Matteo had walked in, Angelo smiled. It wasn't an overly large smile, nor was it a puppy-love smile, but it was one of familiarity. Matteo supposed that was a step forward for the two who had suffered an awkward courtship and even more awkward marriage in order to uphold Isoladian tradition.

"Anything for you." Angelo took the plate and waited until she'd left the room. Then he gobbled up a whole cookie in a very un-princely like manner.

"Calm down. No one will take them from you," Matteo teased.

Angelo dropped to the couch, holding the plate under his chin as he started on another treat. "Aria banned all sweets from the suite. I haven't had sugar in a month." He closed his eyes and moaned. "This must be heaven, because I'm almost glad you came."

Matteo smirked. "Wait—I've seen you at state dinners. They serve dessert." He sat next to Angelo and slung his arm over the back of the couch, settling in as if he weren't about to drop a bomb on Angelo's world.

"I promised Aria that I wouldn't eat it if she couldn't eat it. She's so worried about this baby that she'd gone all organic foods." He took another big bite and moaned. When he opened his eyes, he glanced down at the cookie in his hand. "Who made these?"

"The American had a baking party with Carlotta and Emmilia this evening before their dancing lesson."

"Why?"

"Because she's kind and wanted to make their holiday special."

"By teaching them menial tasks?"

"Since when are you such an elitist?" Matteo instantly regretted his rough tone. He was here to gain his brother's support in a Christmas marriage coup; he needed to make friends, not make them angry. "Sorry. I know you don't see the value in cooking, but the girls had a wonderful time. It was also a chance for them to give back to the people who serve them all year. There are over a dozen plates of cookies being enjoyed, thanks to those three lovely ladies."

Angelo's chewing slowed, and he studied Matteo out of the corner of his eye. "Why do I feel like I just ate a bribe?"

Matteo laughed. "No bribe. A gift. *Signorina* Avery simply wanted to express her gratitude for the gracious way you opened our home to a group of stranded travelers."

Angelo brushed the crumbs off his fingers. There were three cookies left on the plate, but he set it aside. "You are using her first name?"

"*Si.*"

Angelo pressed his palms together and tapped his hands against his lips. "And how are things with Luciana? Are you on a first-name basis with her?"

"I am not." Matteo leaned forward, his elbows on his knees. "I do not love her, brother. And I fear she would not do well at my side. We think differently on important issues."

Angelo glanced toward the doorway where

Aria had disappeared. "It's not about getting along—not at first. Love can come later."

"Perhaps." Matteo also glanced over his shoulder at the doorway. "I seem to remember cold feet on your part. Have you come to love your wife?"

Angelo regarded him coolly. "If you were anyone but my brother, I would throw you out in the snow just for asking that question."

"You can try." Matteo cracked his knuckles.

Angelo waved him off. "I'm growing to love Aria. With every day we plan for our child, I'm drawn to her. I believed she was a follower, someone who would stand beside me and champion my efforts. I've learned that she is a quiet leader, and I find myself turning to her more often for advice and counsel. I respect her, and admire her, and feel the stirrings of something much deeper inside of my heart. In time, I believe I will love her beyond what I ever thought possible."

"I'm happy for you."

"But you do not believe a similar fate awaits you with Luciana?"

"I think one of us would murder the other within the first year."

Angelo burst out a laugh. "I wonder who would draw first."

Matteo sat taller. "Probably her, because we both know I cannot keep my mouth shut. All joking aside, I cannot propose to her on Christmas Eve. I feel as though it would be a death knell for my soul."

"You have to." Angelo's tone brokered no argument.

And yet, all it did was add lighter fluid to Matteo's fiery thoughts. "I won't."

Angelo jerked as if he'd been struck. While he had the kingly attribute of speaking as if his word were law, Matteo had the ability to say words that struck to the heart of an issue. It was that striking that often got him in trouble. However, when one was raised by a king, one had to know how to stand tall—even in the face of a blizzard.

"I came to ask for your help."

Angelo leapt to his feet and paced in front of Matteo. His face drew into a scowl, and his hands dug into his hips. "You want me to thwart a hundred-year-old tradition—before I'm crowned king?"

"Yes."

"*Sei fuori de testa?*"

"No, for the first time, I feel like I'm in my

right mind." He pushed off and stopped Angelo's pacing. "I do not want to be a puppet. My happiness is the one thing that is my own. I will protect it."

"At what cost to the rest of your family? To our country? Are you truly going to be that selfish?"

Matteo's shoulders slumped forward. Selfish. A word akin to treason in the castle. "In this area, I feel I must."

Angelo sighed and placed a hand on his shoulder, forcing him to look up. "You are more than this, little brother. Do not fall into a trap."

Matteo leaned back, unwilling to get drawn into Angelo's pretense of brotherhood and comfort. "What trap?"

"Beautiful women can snare a man with nothing more than a look." He picked up a cookie. "And this one has tricks you are not prepared against."

"It is a cookie," he argued.

"Is that all it is?" He crumbled it in his fist, letting the bits fall to the carpet.

Matteo shook his head, thinking of the maid who would have to clean that up. Angelo surely wouldn't. "She is different, but that does not mean she is bad."

"If she cares about you, she will want to see you do your duty to your family and country." Angelo placed his arm around Matteo's shoulders and walked him to the door. "Listen to my advice: do not spend another moment with *Signorina* Avery. Wash her from your thoughts and focus on the Christmas Eve ball. The more time you focus on what is important, the easier it will be to see that she is not meant for this life."

Matteo gritted his teeth. She may not have been raised in a castle, but she was a good person, wholesome even. Besides, it wasn't about if she could be a princess; it was about the place she had found in his thoughts. Not to mention the place she could take in his heart. It would be easy to fall in love with a woman like Avery.

Very easy indeed.

CHAPTER 13

AVERY

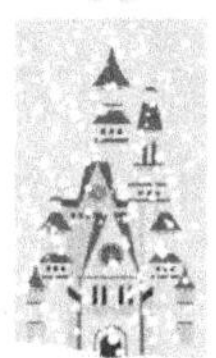

Avery's small room in the servant quarters was cozy and warm as she shared cocoa and store-bought cookies with Brandy and talked over the evening. She should have kept some of the cookies she'd made with Matteo and his sisters, but she'd given them all away. "I mean, at first I thought he was this stuffy butler guy, but he's … sweet. You should have seen him with his sisters—it's adorable." She placed a hand over her heart and sighed.

"And also, he's not a butler." Brandy repositioned herself so that she was sideways on her bed with her back against the wall.

"Right—although I wouldn't mind if he was." Avery held the warm mug in her palms, letting the heat lull her. There seemed to be many sides to Matteo. She couldn't imagine growing up in a place where your life was planned out for you, even if there was comfort in knowing what was expected of you. She'd thought she had a life like that, where holidays were spent at her parents' house, one day bringing children and a husband along. She envied him in some ways.

Brandy grinned wickedly over her cup. "I snuck out while you were baking up a storm with your handsome royal advisor."

Avery perked up. It wasn't like they were trapped here, but with the weather outside so frightful, the castle was surely delightful. "Oh? Where did you go?"

"The gardens." She sighed heavily. "Even in winter, they're beautiful. I swear, one day I'm going to have a shrub-lined path and rosebushes and everything."

"I thought you were going to take the city by storm." They'd had big dreams in college, plans to be the biggest and brightest stars in the cityscape.

"I know I used to say that, but this tour … I don't know. I see all these people taking life at a slower pace, and I'm drawn to it. I feel peaceful here. Don't you?"

Avery dipped a cookie into her cocoa. "It's been nice to be away from familiar things."

"How so?"

"Back home, everywhere I looked were reminders of what I'd lost. But here, I'm not anyone's daughter or student or whatever. I'm just me. At first, it was scary, but I like me." She looked up, hoping for understanding. Brandy was her dearest friend and the closest thing to family on this planet. If anyone would get what she was saying and feeling, it was her. "I'm glad we came. I may not have a savings account anymore, but I'd gladly pay for the kind of closure I've gained."

"So you're good?" Brandy asked with a hearty dash of skepticism.

Avery chuckled. No one could be completely good after the year she'd been through. "I don't know about that. But I do feel like I've found a new normal. Which is funny, because nothing about this trip is normal." She threw a hand out, indicating their surroundings. "We're in a castle for Christmas!" She laughed. "And I baked in a kitchen that was bigger than my whole apartment back home. We didn't even have measuring cups. I had to eyeball the ingredients."

Brandy laughed too, and then she grew contemplative. "You seem really into this guy."

Avery lifted a shoulder while she smiled big. "If he sent me an invitation to meet under the mistletoe, I would RSVP like that." She snapped her fingers. For a moment there, she'd thought Matteo was going to kiss her. Then he'd said that line about how beautiful she was … after walking through a greenhouse and her hair frizzing out, not to mention the flour fight she'd had with the girls. She'd come home looking like she'd wrestled with the Pillsbury Doughboy and he'd come out on top.

Even though she knew it was a line, she believed him. He was just so darn real, it was hard not to. Which was why she'd moved away from a kiss. One touch of his lips and she'd lose all rational thought—not to mention her heart. Which she was just starting to piece back together.

"Okay, but don't give him your heart, please. I don't want to have to haul a puddle of tears back home."

Avery smiled. "I'm just having fun on my once-in-a-lifetime European adventure with my best friend. My heart is safe." She took a sip, using the cup to hide her face. Her emotions were near the surface too often to mask them. Matteo was unlike any man she'd ever met. It would be easy to get caught up in the romance of castle life paired with his good looks and charming smile.

Brandy was right, though. They were leaving as soon as the airport reopened. There was no sense falling for a man who was tied to this island when she had a plane ticket home. Not that she had anything more than a half-baked job and an empty house waiting for her. If he asked her to … No. She couldn't go down that road. They were enjoying time together—brief, noncommittal time that was so wonderful she wished she could bottle it up to open later.

"So what's next?" Brandy asked before throwing back what was left in her mug.

"We're building a snowman tomorrow."

"Fun. Oh!" Her eyes lit up, and she hugged her mug to her chest. "I almost forgot to tell you. Since the storm is so bad, the castle is short-staffed for the holidays, and they're all stressed out. They've asked if we would set up for the dinner tomorrow night and then serve at the Christmas Eve ball the next. They'll pay us for our time, even though they're not charging us for rooms or rent or anything. Isn't that great?"

"That's really kind of them. I hope you signed me up."

"You know I did. This is going to be sick. I can't believe we actually get to go to the ball."

Avery held her cup in the space between them. "To Isola de la Familia."

"To Isola." Brandy clicked her mug against Avery's.

She might not be able to take a royal advisor home, but she planned to enjoy every moment she had with him in the castle.

CHAPTER 14

MATTEO

"This would be easier if you all helped instead of laughing at me." His arms were stretched across a large snowball that he was trying to roll up the side of an even larger snowball to form a snowman. He had it halfway there but couldn't seem to get a good grip to push it the rest of the way.

The trouble was, the thing was dashedly heavy and slippery to boot. His face was red with exertion, and his legs ached. If he wasn't careful, he'd throw his back out.

It might be worth it to get out of the Christmas Eve ball, but not even an injury would keep his father from stuffing him into a tuxedo and pronouncing him engaged. No doubt Angelo would help Padre, the traitor.

His sisters and Avery stood several feet away, giggling over the absurd position he'd gotten himself into.

Still laughing, Avery came to his side. "I'd help, but I'm just not sure where to …" She approached his right side, but his leg and arm were in the way of her grabbing hold. She went around to the left and found the same problem. "Maybe if we …" She went behind him and leaned into his back, digging her feet into the deep snow. This, in turn, pushed his chest against the snowball and held it in place. "Better?"

In some ways, yes. The snowball stayed put. But with her body pressed to his, even with the layers and layers of clothing they wore to keep warm, Matteo was ultimately distracted from his goal. All he wanted to do was turn and take Avery in his arms. "*Signorina,* I find myself caught between a snowball and a beautiful woman. Was it your intent to trap me here?"

She giggled softly and lifted her chin to rest on his shoulder. "I'm not the kind of woman who has to trap a man." Her breath was warm on his cheek and sent a thrill through him.

"I believe you've trapped many a heart in your

day, *signorina*. Though you may not have been aware of it at the time." She'd certainly laid snares for him today.

It had all started when she'd appeared wearing a stocking hat and two long braids—like a schoolgirl. Only, she was all woman in her fitted coat and tight pants. He liked a lady with curves, and she had them in all the right places. He found her a sweet concoction of innocence and seduction and instantly knew she was unaware of her own charms.

Her feminine traps had continued as she'd tromped through the gardens with his sisters, looking for the perfect spot to build their project. She'd held their mittened hands, listened to their lamentations over dance class the night before, and made a snow angel right beside them. Which was more than incredible, because his little sisters didn't often have the opportunity to be children.

Avery's time spent in their world made an impact on his heart—one he couldn't ignore.

With the added leverage, Matteo found that he could drop his arms lower. "That's good. On three, push up." He counted, and she pressed up and into him. With much effort, he was able to finally get the snowman put together.

His sisters cheered.

"I forgot the scarf!" Carlotta bemoaned. "Come on." She grabbed Emmilia's hand. "We'll get it and be right back."

"*Si*. But don't let *Bambiana* see us, or we'll be forced into tea," Emmilia cautioned.

Avery shooed them with her hands. "Hurry back. We can't finish him without you."

They rushed off, kicking snow up behind their boots like racehorses.

"They're so cute." Avery hugged herself.

Matteo joined her in watching them scamper off. His breath came in short puffs, but he wasn't sure if that was the exercise or Avery's nearness. "They are pests and have far too much energy for the household—but I wouldn't have them any other way."

She stepped back with her hands on her hips to preview their work. "It's not bad. Leans a bit to the left."

Matteo looked up to see that the snowman was several inches taller than him and it did in fact lean.

Avery must have seen him measuring himself to a giant snow-blob, because she cocked her head and gave him a little smirk. "You aren't jealous of him, are you?"

"Why would I be jealous?"

"Well, because he's so well shaped." She made a big circle with her arms. "Obviously."

"I have always believed myself to be of a good *shape*, as you call it."

She eyed him, being obvious in her perusal. He folded his hands behind his back and lifted his chin.

"Meh," she offered before reaching out to smooth off some of the snowman's rough edges.

"Meh? Meh!" He grabbed her around the middle and spun her around, pinning her against his chest. He'd never taken such liberties with a woman, and yet it all felt so natural. "Never, in all my life, has anyone described me as *meh*."

She giggled. "What do they call you, then?"

"Handsome. Charming. A regular prince of a guy."

Their gazes collided, and she stilled in his arms. "See, now, that's where they were wrong." Her voice was low, barely meeting his ears. With careful movements, she slid her hands up his chest and wrapped her arms around his neck. "You, Matteo, are anything but regular."

"I do not feel *regular* when I am around you." He leaned closer, his eyes dropping to trace the bow of her bottom lip. She tipped her head up in invitation. "I feel like a king," he mumbled.

She lifted onto her toes, and their mouths came together. He wasn't sure if he meant to kiss her; he'd like to think that he had the guts to go for it. But she could very well claim that she'd kissed him first. Which didn't sit right.

And so he set out to make up for his hesitation by pulling her body flush with his and deepening the kiss. As he did, the strangest thing happened inside of him. It was as if his whole life he'd been waiting for this moment—waiting to hold this woman close, to taste the mint on her tongue that was as cool as the air around them, and yet she was as warm as a fire on a winter's day.

He'd found his other half. The knowledge was like a bolt of lightning to his heart, and he nearly staggered under the blow.

Avery's eyes fluttered open, and she looked up at him. "That was anything but regular."

He grinned. "*Sono d'accordo.*"

A happy shriek filled the air, alerting them to the dramatic and loud approach of his little sisters. As much as he would have loved to stand there, holding Avery and exploring her lips for the rest of the morning, he needed some time to absorb the knowledge and feelings growing inside of him. He slowly removed his arms, and she tucked her hands into her pockets, silently agreeing that what had happened would stay between the two of them for now.

"Matteo!" Emmilia yelled as she careened around the hedge and into view. "Madre came out with us." Her little cherub cheeks were flushed with the cold and happiness.

A moment later, Madre and Carlotta appeared, carrying a picnic basket between them. Madre didn't falter at the sight of Avery nor the snowman, which meant that his sisters had done a fine job of filling her in on their morning adventures.

He hurried over to drop a kiss on his mother's cheek and take the basket. "What's in here?" He pretended to be dragged down by the basket. He then reached over and felt Carlotta's muscles, making her laugh out loud.

"It's a tea service," Carlotta replied as if admonishing him for his silliness.

He didn't care if his little sister thought she was more mature than him. At the moment, he could roll in the snow like a puppy and not care. Avery had kissed him! He could fly over the castle if he wanted to.

Madre assessed the spot they'd chosen to build the snowman. The tall hedges gave them privacy and some protection from the wind. The blizzard continued to pound areas of Isola, but the high castle walls proved an asset against the storm. Instead of snow coming at them sideways, as it did on the new reports, it fell with relative gentleness.

"Would you set that on the bench for us, *polpetto?*"

He glanced at Avery to see if she'd heard his mother's term of endearment. Being called *meatball* wasn't too bad in the privacy of the family setting, but in front of a woman he was trying to impress, it was rather embarrassing.

She winked at him, and her eyes sparkled with a future round of teasing. He grinned back. Teasing was quickly becoming one of his favorite pastimes, and now that he'd kissed her, he could work some of that into their verbal sparring as well. Indeed, the prospect was enjoyable enough to have him trip over his own feet on the way to the bench.

"Before we have tea, this snowman needs a proper dressing," Madre pronounced.

"Did you find the coins?" Avery asked Emmilia, who shook her head.

"Madre brought some, though."

Madre pulled several shiny gold coins from her pocket.

Avery stepped forward to look. "Why coins? We use buttons and coal."

"It's tradition." Emmilia took one of them, and Matteo lifted her up so she could make it into an eye.

Madre picked up Avery's education on the history of the coins and snowmen. "When the snow melts, the coins are lost. But if you find one in the spring or summer, then it will bring you luck until the first snowfall."

Avery lowered her eyebrows. "Didn't people steal them?"

"No!" Carlotta shook her head so hard her hat dislodged.

Madre reached over to fix it. "Stealing a coin brings a year of shame and bad luck to the thief."

"And their family," added Emmilia in all seriousness.

"Not even a disgruntled prince would dare risk the curse upon his father's head." Madre gave Matteo a look, and he quickly got to work adding coins from his own pocket to the front of the snowman. Hopefully, Avery didn't figure out that Madre was talking about him.

"Perhaps it is not a question of being disgruntled as much as it is a sense of being measured." He tried to veil his response, but Avery was listening closely.

Madre pressed her lips together—a sign that she worked to control her emotions and speak with diplomacy.

Avery looked back and forth between the two of them. "Maybe everyone—" She gave him a pointed look. "—would be happier if they stopped measuring and worrying over the results, and started living."

"Is that what you do?" Madre asked, her royal brow arched in suspicion.

Avery ducked and studied her gloves. "It's what I wished I'd done while my parents were alive."

Madre's arched brow dropped. "You are an orphan."

Avery blew out a breath. "I'm still coming to terms with that label. It feels stark, and it's one I didn't ask for, but yes."

"Do you have siblings?" Madre's voice and posture softened. She studied Avery as if seeing her in a new light. Matteo tried to see what she did. A woman who was alone in the world, setting out to explore it rather than being afraid. Someone who had every right to point to herself and demand others take care of her, but who had gone and made his sisters' Christmas all the brighter.

"No." Avery dropped her chin. "It's just me now."

Such a big answer in one little word. Matteo's breath caught. She truly had no one in this world. Even when he didn't like his father's proclamations, he knew that he had family.

Madre must have come to the same conclusion, because she reached out and touched Avery's arm—a grand statement of acceptance from the queen. "I am so sorry for your loss."

Avery smiled sadly. "Thank you. This is my first Christmas without my parents." She smiled at them, even the girls, who were building a mini snowman to go with the larger one. "But your family has made it so I'm not alone."

"We are glad you are with us." Madre's eyes brightened. "You should come to the ball."

Matteo drew back in surprise. The ball was for dignitaries and royals—not for orphaned Americans snowed in at the castle. His gaze jumped to Madre's, searching for something. There! He caught the acceptance, the admiration in Madre's gaze. He felt the breath go out of him. Madre *liked* her. He didn't know quite what it was that Avery had done, but it endeared her to the queen. Matteo gave Madre a look of gratitude. She gave him a look that said, *Don't make a big deal out of it.*

Avery laughed. "I don't think that will work. I don't have a dress or anything."

Madre tossed her concern aside. "The girls' dresses are done, and the seamstresses would love to create something for you."

Avery's forehead wrinkled. "I don't want to be a bother."

Matteo touched her elbow. "Come," he pleaded.

She seemed to be at war with herself. "But I signed up to serve at the ball. I don't want to leave them high and dry."

"I'll personally make sure they have enough staff." He made an X over his chest.

"Okay," she whispered in reply. An alarm sounded on her phone, and she jolted. "Where has the time gone?" She stepped back and smiled at all of them. "I have to go. I promised I'd be somewhere. I'm so sorry."

Matteo took her hand and bowed over it. "Tomorrow is Christmas Eve. Would you go on a sleigh ride with me?"

She blushed. "I'd like that." Her phone beeped,

and her forehead wrinkled. "That's probably Brandy. I really do have to go."

She slipped her hand out of his and waved to the girls before hurrying around the shrub.

Madre came to stand beside him. "I have not seen you this animated, Matteo. That woman affects you."

"That she does, Madre." He turned so he faced her. "I think she would make an excellent partner in life."

Madre nodded sagely.

"You are not surprised?"

"I felt the charge between you two the moment I stepped into this clearing." She removed her glove and cupped his cheek. "I fear the path you are insistent on following is rough and will cause you to trip and fall. As a mother, I do not want to see you suffer."

"Then stand with me as I fight for the chance to love the person I choose."

"Will she stand with you? Will she be firm as the press calls her every dirty name in the book? As our sister nations question not only our commitment to our way of life but your commitment to Isola? Will she stand by you if your father disowns you and strips you of your title?"

"He would not." Matteo could see Padre doing many things, but taking public action against his son was not one of them.

"He may be forced to, if the people insist upon it. Isola is nothing if it isn't traditional. We are one of the few nations in the world who take such pride in the old ways while moving into the next century. With so many changes happening in the world, our people long for simpler times when their princes obeyed the king."

He sighed. "Why does being royal have to complicate falling in love?"

Madre burst out a laugh that startled the girls. "*Polpetto*, love is complicated for everyone. Being royal has nothing to do with it."

He smiled at her gentle rebuke.

"I am on your side and will do what I can to help your father see reason." She drew in a breath. "But it will take a miracle to bring us through this as a family. I will pray to Saint Joseph that he will allow us to pass through troubled waters unscathed."

"I suppose I should pray too."

"*Polpetto*, you have bigger problems."

"I do?"

"You need to get that sweet American to fall in

love with you as much as you are in love with her."

He grinned, thinking of their kiss. "I'll work on that."

She nodded once. "See that you do. Now, I'm getting chilly and would like some tea."

"Yes, Madre."

Matteo called the girls over, and his mother poured tea. She regaled them with stories from her childhood and the games she'd played with her brothers growing up in the countryside.

Matteo half listened to the stories and half plotted how he would show Avery that they were meant to be together. A future with her seemed bright and beautiful. Well, the part after the wedding. Everything leading up to that was going to be an uphill climb. If she loved him, really and truly loved him, she'd climb that mountain too. But if she didn't? Well, then he might as well marry Luciana, because no one would ever compare to Avery.

CHAPTER 15

AVERY

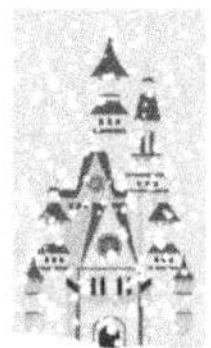

"Where have you been?" hissed Brandy.

Avery scooted in beside her, pushing a cart full of silverware and napkins. The rest of their group pushed similar carts with plates of varying sizes, glasses, and napkin rings.

"You missed the orientation."

"I know. Sorry. I got caught up with—" Her eyes darted to Tina, who was walking in front of them but leaning back so she could listen in on the conversations. "—my friend."

"*Caught up* caught up? Or just distracted?" Brandy pumped her eyebrows.

"Caught up," Avery squealed as quietly as possible.

Brandy hip-bumped her. "Way to go."

They reached the formal dining room and an impossibly thin doorway. Sabrina held up a hand for them to stop, as if they would have gone right through the walls without her direction. "This door and that one down there are the only entrances for the staff. You will wait on this side of the door for everyone who needs to get out. Leaving the room is the priority—no matter how hot the dish you carry."

"I doubt they believe in pot holders," Brandy whispered.

"I thought we weren't serving, just setting up?"

"The guys were asked to serve. Seems they were short a few men. They were fitted for the proper attire this morning while you were out melting snow with your *friend*."

Avery smirked. Melting snow was an understatement. Kissing Matteo was unlike any kissing experience she'd had thus far, and she doubted she'd ever have its equal again. Sigh. The troubles of an international traveler who must return home to a job she didn't want in a city she didn't care to live in. Going home looked less and less appealing.

"There is a diagram on the top of your cart.

Stay in line and follow it." Sabrina opened the door with a flourish.

From the back, Avery couldn't see what all the gasping and exclaiming were about. When it was finally her and Brandy's turn to walk in, her mouth fell to the floor. "You know, I get that we're staying in a castle, but sometimes, I'm blown away." They walked forward, their eyes on everything but where they were going, and they bumped into Tina.

"Sorry," Avery and Brandy chorused.

"No worries. I can hardly believe this place."

"It's magical." Avery tipped her head back and took in the crystal chandeliers that danced light throughout the room like a choreographer in a ballroom. The windows were five feet wide and twelve feet tall, allowing for a stunning view overlooking the city of Isola below.

"I'd forgotten we were on a hill," said Stacy as she looked from the view down to the diagram on her cart. The boys laid out the white plates and glasses, and the girls were to follow with the silverware.

Sabrina stopped in front of them. "Placement must be precise and universal. The younger prince is expected to propose to the woman of his choice at the Christmas Eve ball. This dinner is the opening event to Christmas in the castle and must be absolutely perfect."

"So we gotta make this look good," Stacy quipped back at her.

Sabrina smirked. "Yes. I asked you ladies to do it, because I believe you have an eye for detail that your male counterparts lack." She rotated slightly so they could see the guys rushing through the process of stacking plates atop the charger with a beautiful filigree in blue and gold around the edges. "I'll follow behind them and ensure that the plates are aligned."

Avery smiled at Sabrina's sense of long-suffering with the men in their group. She'd seen some of the same in Matteo's mother as she'd talked with her son. It must be an Isoladian female trait.

Tina went first, loading the left side of the plate with the salad and dinner forks. Stacy came behind her, putting the butter knife on the right. Brandy followed, adding the dinner fork and spoon below the plate stack, with the handles facing opposite directions. Avery came last, rolling the napkins, folding them in half, and sliding a silver napkin ring with the royal crest on it before placing them just so on top of the plates. They didn't try to hurry along but worked steadily. The guys finished up, and Sabrina whisked them off for instructions on serving drinks after dinner.

"Can you believe we'll be here when the prince gets engaged?" Tina sighed deeply. "It's so romantic."

"So's Avery sneaking off to meet some guy," said Stacy with a knowing smile. "I think it's about time we get some details."

"Who says I'm meeting a guy?" Avery replied, content not to make her social life the topic of conversation. Besides, there was something fun about sneaking around. It wasn't like the other girls hadn't snuck out to meet a guy at one time or another during their tour. Of course, they always dished about their romantic adventures and Avery had listened with rapt attention. It felt like everyone else's lives were more interesting than hers. Until now.

Stacy paused just long enough to pin Avery with a look. "Come on. I saw you ducking out this morning. No one looks over their shoulder unless there's a secret meeting going on. Spill."

"Yeah." Tina nodded in agreement. "I told you about the French guy."

"Following a man up the Eiffel Tower to check off your bucket kissing-list is hardly the same thing as—" Avery came up short, aware that she'd already revealed more than she wanted to.

"Oh my gosh! You like this guy." Stacy fanned her face.

"Guys, come on." Brandy motioned for Stacy and Tina to keep moving. She'd caught up and had to wait for them to get their jobs done.

Avery appreciated the respite she'd managed to gain. But it wasn't meant to last.

"Come on, just share the best part." Tina set a salad fork, eyed its spot, and moved it down a fraction.

Avery debated whether or not she should say anything, but then she finally decided that she could tell them what they'd already find out anyway. "He works in the castle—hence we met here. And he invited me to the ball."

"Yeah, we're all going. As. Servers." Tina continued down the row.

"No. As a guest." She hugged herself. "The whole thing feels so unreal. I'm getting a ball gown and everything." The words tumbled out of her, and with them, the happiness bubbled it. Like shaking a soda and then opening the lid. She had no control over how much she spoke; even if she put her hand over the top to stop talking, it just kept going. "It's all planned out. His dad is an advisor to the king, and his mom arranged things with the royal seamstress."

"What?" Stacy shrieked, the sound echoing off the glass windows.

Avery and Brandy laughed at her outrage.

She glared. "That is *so* not fair."

"Life isn't fair." Brandy gave Stacy a look that said back-off-my-friend's-been-through-crap-and-deserves-this.

Avery touched Brandy's arm. "It's fine. I'd be jealousy too. I'm not trying to brag—I'm just so happy."

Stacy wrenched her gaze away and set her next knife down, hard. She mumbled something under her breath that Avery chose not to try to decipher. Jealousy didn't bear sweet fruits.

Brandy smiled funny, like she wasn't sure she'd heard her right.

Avery dropped her head back and laughed. "I feel happy. It's wonderful and strange, and I think I might cry." She swiped at the moisture leaking from her eyes even as she kept laughing. "I didn't think I would feel like this ever again, and to feel it over a *dress?* That's just crazy."

"I don't think it's the dress." Brandy hugged her, rubbing her back. "You deserve to be happy

—remember that." She let her go and started back on her job.

"Well, I'm happy for you," said Tina. "Vacation flings are fun. You get some good kissing in and then get to leave town."

At first, all Avery could think about was the way it felt the moment Matteo had taken control of their kiss. He was so … commanding and sure and just plain manly. She'd had no defense, no strength, no power to resist him. Heaven help her, he was such a good kisser. Avery threw up her hands. "It doesn't feel like a fling. Like Stacy said, I like him." Holy Toledo, she liked Matteo—a lot. Like *a lot* a lot. Like more than she'd ever like a man before. She was in new territory with this one.

"Would you marry him?" asked Tina. "Because there was no way I was going to marry Luis. He was cute and all, but he was not the man for me."

Avery grinned. The man had been insufferable, telling Tina she was more beautiful every moment she was on his arm. Maybe he didn't have a good grasp of the language and American idioms, but he'd often come off sounding chauvinistic. By the time they'd left Madrid, all the women in the group had been happy to be rid of him.

"Well?" Tina pressed.

Avery chewed her lip. "From what I've seen, he's loyal, dedicated to his family and country, and has a determination that makes me think he could be anything he wants to be."

"But does he shake your Christmas tree?" Stacy pumped her eyebrows.

Did he ever! He shook her tree, melted her inner snow woman, and jiggled her jingle bells. Avery laughed and shook her shoulders, "There's a whole lotta shakin' going on."

The girls laughed.

Stacy bumped her cart ahead with her hip as she worked. "Well, don't get too attached. He got into this knowing you were leaving town; he may think it's a fling, even if you don't."

"Stacy, I'm sure this guy is as into Avery just as much as she's into him." Brandy turned toward Avery and made a face.

Avery smiled in gratitude but then turned to keep her eyes on her work. Was Matteo only flirting with her because she was here for the short term? The thought didn't sit right, and she adjusted her neck against the tight and uncomfortable feelings it created. They'd only known each other for a couple days, but the time they spent together was set apart, different from other moments of her day. It was like stepping into shallow water knowing you were going to wade all the way into the ocean at some point.

Frustration built inside of her. It wasn't like she could drop a *where do you think this is going* question on him after one kiss. She suddenly wished the storm would never stop and she and Matteo would have months together to figure this out.

Because he hadn't asked her to stay, nor did she have any evidence that he would.

Neither could she ask him to go; his family was here, his job, his life. If one of them were to relocate, it would have to be her. She would, though. Which was totally scary but also amazing. She looked around the dining room and wondered what it would be like to live here, to be a part of something that had been around longer than the state she currently called home.

To belong.

The thought was overwhelming and caused her eyes to burn with unshed tears. As much as she wanted that feeling, she wanted Matteo more. She prayed he didn't think they were a vacation fling, because there was a feast laid before her and she was starving. If he took it away, it could ruin her forever.

The trouble was, she had no way to protect her heart. She didn't know how. She was made to love, and she couldn't stop herself any more than she could stop the snow from falling. The best she could do was hope Matteo would be there to catch her and that she didn't end up shattering.

CHAPTER 16

MATTEO

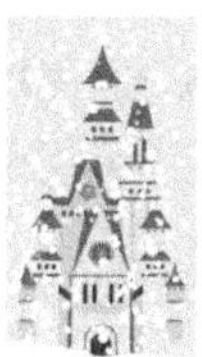

"You must approve the place setting."

"I already did. White plates—remember?" Matteo followed behind Alfredo, his mind only half consumed with plans for the Christmas celebrations he was over. The other half was back in the garden, holding Avery and exploring her lips in a dedicated fashion.

"That was plates; this is the full setting. And the ballroom decorations need your keen eye." Alfredo clasped his hands behind his back.

"You and I both know I do not have talent in decorating nor judging whether decorations are appropriate."

Alfredo's face remained neutral. He would never say a bad word about Matteo—though he'd been known to correct him on more than one occasion. In private. With decorum. "A prince's duty is not to know everything, but to manage those who do."

"It's interesting to get these little glimpses into the way you view my life." Matteo slapped him on the back, causing him to grunt.

They were coming upon the entrance to the dining room. The twelve-foot doorway was swathed in boughs decorated with ribbons of blue and silver, denoting the royal colors. The doors were thrown wide open in greeting, a feeling he thought appropriate. The guests for the ball who'd managed to make it to Isola before the storm hit were put up in local inns or the castle itself. Though he'd had little to do with them as they were kept apart from his family, tonight's dinner was the official opening event for Christmas in the castle.

He stopped outside the door and ran his eyes along the trim. "I used to love this archway as a child. Going through it felt as though I was stepping into another land." He stopped to turn to Alfredo. "I believe the decorations had much to do with that feeling, and these do not disappoint. You may give my compliments to the designer."

Alfredo's smile was one of satisfaction, though

Matteo wasn't sure if he was more pleased with the way the doorway turned out or the way he had. Heaven knew the man had a heavy hand in raising him. Perhaps that was why Matteo bristled so under his father's dictates. A part of him didn't believe the man had earned the right to tell him what to do.

And yet he was king and had every right. Matteo would do well to remember that, even if it raked against his skin, because it seemed like he spoke more often to his king than his *padre* these days.

Soft voices and the tinkling of silverware and napkin rings on plates met his ear. He focused on the crew at the other end of the room and jolted. Avery was here. He jumped and pressed his back to the open door, afraid she or one of the others had seen him.

Alfredo raised an eyebrow. "Did you see a spider, *principe?*"

"Shh." Matteo motioned for him to get out of the doorway. He moved, albeit slower than honey in December. Once Alfredo was out of the way, he whispered, "Avery's in there."

"And you do not wish to see her? I was under the impression you couldn't get enough of her time." He picked an imaginary piece of lint off his jacket.

"I would very much like to march in there and sweep her away, but Sabrina is there. She knows I'm a prince."

Alfredo took a peek around the corner of the doorway. Matteo grabbed his jacket and pulled him back and tucking him on the other side— away from the open door.

"I hate to break it to you, *principe*, but the entire world knows you are a prince."

"Not Avery." He flipped so his front was to the door and peeked around the pine boughs. "She thinks I am a royal advisor."

"And you thought it was wise to allow her this disillusion … why?" His voice dripped with disdain. Apparently, Alfredo was on team Avery. At the rate she acquired admirers, she'd have the whole castle on her side. Which was great, except they'd all look at him like Alfredo was looking at him—like he wanted to send him to time out in the dungeons—for lying to the girl.

He sighed and rested his forehead against the wood. "Because she would have treated me different if she knew."

Alfredo grunted. "I believe you have underestimated the woman."

Had he? Probably. But what was he to do about it now? His father was breathing down his neck to marry another woman. Luciana was already campaigning for the pet projects she wanted to take on when she was a princess. His brother was ready to wrestle him into doing his duty to God and country. The only ones on his side were his mother, his younger sisters, Alfredo, and everyone who'd tasted her cookies.

He thought about what he would say, but none of it made a difference, because as a prince, he wasn't free to give his heart. At least as an advisor, he could pursue the woman of his dreams. "I don't want her to know I'm the prince until I can offer her more."

"More what?" Alfredo asked as if there was nothing more valuable than his title—though Matteo knew he didn't think that.

"More than cookies and a snowman."

"Christmas Eve is tomorrow."

"Must you remind me of the deadline? I'm working on it," he ground out. He was working on it. Changing traditions took time—which he didn't have much of. But Madre was quietly working behind the scenes on Padre today. He had to give her a chance to lay a foundation he could build on. "Come. Let us check the ballroom." He darted across the opening, praying the chatty women at the other end didn't see him dash by. Or, if they did, that Avery didn't recognize him.

Alfredo harrumphed and walked as if everything in his world were on even keel.

Matteo wished he had that luxury, but he was thwarting tradition and his father's wishes. Even keel was as far away as Australia.

CHAPTER 17

MATTEO

With each bite he took during the antipasti, Matteo couldn't help but think of Avery. Had she touched this fork? This plate? When he'd seen her earlier, she'd been rolling napkins. He held his napkin ring until Madre looked pointedly at it and then at the table, telling him to put it down as she had when he was a fidgeting child.

He winked at her as he slipped it into his pocket, where it would be close to his heart, and tuned into the conversation going on around him.

Padre and Madre sat at the head of the table. Angelo was on Padre's right, and Matteo was on

Madre's left. Aria was next to Angelo, and then Luciana and her padre the *marchese*. He wasn't in charge of the seating chart—that was Madre's doing. He wished he'd taken a moment to consider the arrangement before he was across from his would-be princess. Moving her down the table would have been a slight but also a warning shot across the bow that she hadn't secured the position she counted on.

To Matteo's right was Isola's prime minister, Signora Manichi, and her husband was next to her. If there was conversation down the table, it was spoken too quietly for the royal family to participate in—which was considered polite but also made for a boring evening.

Padre stood and held up his glass. "To my son, Matteo, for planning a wonderful meal to start out the holiday."

"*Cin cin,*" echoed over 100 guests. More had been invited but were unable to travel. Which allowed for more elbow room during the meal, though Matteo was disappointed that his friends from boarding school, princes in their own right, hadn't been able to make it.

Padre lifted his glass and sipped the amber contents. Matteo stood and bowed to the group, acknowledging their praise.

As he pulled his chair in, his father said, "My sons, you make me proud."

Matteo's head came around, surprised to be included in the speech. Padre didn't say much about him in public, focusing on Angelo and his strides toward becoming king.

"I don't say it enough, but your dedication to Isola and her people makes me proud."

Matteo's smile felt like a ghost on his lips.

Roberto, Luciana's father, leaned slightly forward, indicating that he wished to speak. "I appreciate your attention to tradition, *sua Maesta*. It is the foundation of our strong country."

Matteo barely held back his eye roll. The fact that he did was a testament to his tutors over the years.

Madre kicked him under the table, and he jolted, realizing she wished him to speak up.

He cleared his throat. "Agreed. Our traditions have served us well. But the world is changing quickly around us. Our bees sustain agriculture here and over much of Europe, but how long before someone invents a pollination machine that would put them out of work?"

Luciana gasped, splaying her hand across her chest. "Surely nothing could replace our beloved bees." She glanced right and then left. "They are as respected as the monarchy."

Soft murmurs of approval came from all corners.

"Of course," Matteo placated her. "But we cannot ignore advancement." The prime minister tipped her head toward him as she sliced her beef. He had her ear; now he had to make use of it. "Perhaps we should move Isola forward by evaluating some of the traditions we honor."

"Like what?" asked Madre. She was all innocence and interest, playing along as if she didn't know Matteo had an ulterior motive in this conversation. God bless her.

"For example, allowing those from other nations to marry into our royal family. Maybe even an American."

Padre snorted and joked, "We aren't English, son."

His tone brought out a large guffaw from Roberto, followed quickly by twittering from Luciana. Soon, half the table was laughing at Padre's joke—despite its lack of humor and the fact that they hadn't heard a word. "Laugh when the king laughs" was a banquet rule.

Ridiculous.

But he had bigger fights to fight.

When the clamor died down, Padre pinned Matteo with a look. "Like the bees in our hives, we are strong because we stick together. Any one of us on our own cannot bring success to the nation. But by doing their part, each bee gives strength to the hive."

Matteo pressed his lips into a thin line. "While I appreciate and honor our national symbol, I disagree with your reasoning. A bee may fly with the purpose of making honey, but he is allowed to choose his path, to explore the garden for the sweetest flowers."

Luciana's eyes were large with panic as she seemed to realize he might not fall in line to marry her. "Surely you, of all people, *principe*, understand how important you are to Isola. Your purpose here is to care for our people." She waved her hand down the table, indicating the group gathered to celebrate the start of the Christmas holiday.

He narrowed his eyes, not appreciating her efforts to force him into agreeing with her in a public forum. Her underhanded tactics only cemented his belief that they would not get on together. "It is interesting, Luciana, that after the holiday, you will be free to make your future into what you want it to be. And yet, you seem to withhold the same privilege from me—simply because I was born with a title."

Her false innocence melted. "My title may be less than yours, but it is no less demanding." Her father placed a warning hand on her forearm, but she didn't drop her challenging gaze.

Matteo's lips twitched. He would not be cowed into a marriage with this woman. Nothing between them was official. She didn't have a guarantee of his proposal, and her parents only had vague references from his parents to stand upon. If he walked away from this engagement, she would not be shamed or written off by the press for anything except her own declarations and assumptions. Besides, this was the first time her true colors shone through in front of his family, and he wasn't about to let them miss what they'd chosen for a daughter-in-law.

Padre cleared his throat, a sure sign he wanted Matteo to change the subject. However, Matteo wasn't through making his point. "I believe the prime minister could attest to the fact that changing certain traditions have benefitted our country—as can we all as we recognize the great contributions *she's* made to foreign affairs since *her* appointment. Which—" He held up a finger for emphasis. "—would not have happened had the law not been changed to allow women to hold the position." He smiled at his seatmate. "Tell us, Prime Minister, how do you feel about keeping up with world culture?"

He barely held back his grin as she seemed to gather herself like a dragon drawing a deep breath. Signora Manichi was known for her forward thinking and somewhat radical ways. Appointing her had been a calculated move to appease those who wanted change in politics without overthrowing the government. The next step would be to appoint a cabinet, elected by the people, to rule along with the king and queen. Padre was silent on the possibility.

Signora Manichi swallowed a bite, dabbed her lips, and sipped her wine. "I believe laws and traditions that withhold personal freedoms must be changed. We cannot expect our people to be their best selves if they are not given every opportunity. To do so while hiding behind tradition is cowardly." She lifted an eyebrow at Roberto, daring him to contradict her.

He dropped his eyes to his plate.

Matteo could have kissed her. Instead, he patted her hand. "Well said."

"*Gratzie.*" She was a woman who spoke her mind, despite knowing it would not garner her additional time in office. Instead, she opted to do as much good as she could while she was in power. Matteo applauded her convictions. That was probably why the people, and Padre, looked to her for guidance in navigating world economics. There was something comforting about knowing a person would tell you the truth no matter what.

Her honesty reminded him of Avery. Which was another reason he'd kept his identity from her. He didn't want her to look at him differently. He didn't think he could bear to see that same calculating gleam in her eye that he saw in Luciana's. It would hurt him more than the daggers Padre threw his way for the rest of the meal.

He was fine with those. After all, you couldn't stage a coup without upsetting the king.

However, upsetting Avery, or seeing her morph into a princess wannabe, would cause major damage. His gut said she would never put on airs or seek a position in the monarchy by marrying him, but as he sat among his peers, many of whom had married into their titles, doubt crept in.

He had to believe she was good and pure. Fingering the napkin ring in his breast pocket, he prayed that he'd chosen the right woman to fight for. If not, he'd never marry. Because if Avery wasn't who he thought she was, then there wasn't a woman on earth he could trust.

CHAPTER 18

AVERY

"You are thin, *si*."

Avery yipped as the seamstress pinched her ribs.

"You should eat cookies, not give them away."

Her good-natured grumping told Avery exactly how much she valued the neighborly gift, and it warmed Avery's heart to know that she'd brought some holiday cheer into her life.

Rosa was in her seventies. Like many of the older women in Isola, she wore her gray hair like a badge of honor. Avery admired that about the culture. Wrinkles … a few extra pounds … even a crooked tooth wasn't reason enough to hate yourself as you dressed every morning. They accepted their bodies, flaws and all, and continued on with their day. It was refreshing.

Avery looked at herself in the mirror. Wearing a long slip, she couldn't believe how much her shoulder blades poked out. "It's been a rough year. And then we backpacked across Europe, so there was lots of walking." Also lots of pasta, breads, sodas … the list went on.

"Rough year? Rough years mean you eat more gelato. Where is your mother? I keep feeling I need to ask."

Avery smiled sadly. Strange that Rosa had that question but probably not so strange considering she was in a foreign land, traipsing about with her best friend. "My mother passed away," she said softly, hoping that Rosa wouldn't take the words as a rebuke. That was the funny thing about being the survivor: she worked so hard to make sure people didn't feel uncomfortable around her—even though the accident wasn't her fault.

Rosa's eyes softened. She sat on a stool and dragged the dress across her lap to take in the sides. "*Quando?*"

"March." She wrapped her arms around herself and shivered. "It was a car accident. My father passed too. It's been … a hard year." She flapped her arms out to the side. "I'm afraid there are no other words—English or Italian—that adequately express what I've gone through."

Rosa whipped thread through the satin fabric without looking down. The woman was a master seamstress. "You are a good daughter to remember them with love. They were good people who taught you about love, *si?*"

Avery smiled. "*Si.*"

Rosa stood up quickly, turning the dress right side out as she did so. "Here, you put this on. I adjust."

Avery did as she was told, shimmying into the sultry fabric as if sliding into a warm pool of water. It was exquisite. Dark blue, cobalt, perhaps? The fabric moved, catching the light in the most wonderful way. She twisted around, letting the hem move.

"You can breathe?" Rosa stepped back to take in the fit.

"*Si.* It's tight, but I don't think I'll be breathing much tomorrow night anyway. This whole experience has taken my breath away." She ran her hand down the front of the dress, feeling the tucks and beads brush her palm and wondering what it would feel like to have Matteo hold her close.

Rosa smiled fondly. "I am an old woman—"

Avery opened her mouth to argue the fact but was stopped by a stern look over the top of magnifying spectacles.

"But I know some things." Rosa held up her finger. "*Una,* when a man's mother arranges for you to attend a ball, it is a good sign."

Avery tried to hold back her grin. She'd had the same thought. She'd also countered it with the idea that Matteo's mom had taken pity on her. Either way, she'd ended up in this dress, and that was a blessing, so she was taking it.

"*Due,* when a man follows you around the castle to carry your cookies, he likes you."

At that, Avery laughed happily. "I don't think it started out that way."

"*Si,* but I saw his face, *signorina.* He didn't know what to make of you but wanted to figure you out."

Avery blushed. "You're saying I'm strange."

"I'm saying you're interesting." She pulled Avery's arms out to the side and glanced over the gown. "And in my dress, you are captivating. You will have his heart by the end of the ball, or I will resign as seamstress."

Avery's hands flew to her mouth. "Don't say that. You'll jinx us."

"There's no jinxing from Isola *nonnas,* unless you see us spit on the ground. Then you run because we curse you." Rosa patted Avery's arm, her face growing serious. "Perhaps it is because I am old, but I feel the space between this world and the next grows smaller as time goes by. I become less scared of walking through death's door. It is because of this that I can say your parents are watching over you. I felt them follow you into the studio. They want you to find love."

Avery blushed and glanced down at her bare feet. "It would be lovely if that were true." She didn't dare hope that her parents were involved in her meeting Matteo. If it didn't work out, she didn't want to blame them for a broken heart. But if it were true, then she could have hope that their holiday romance could blossom into more.

"Knock knock." Matteo's deep voice interrupted the expectant silence that had fallen over the work space.

"Ah! *Muovi le gombe,* have you come to torment me with your fidgeting?" Rosa lifted up to plant a grandmotherly kiss on Matteo's cheek.

He chuckled in response to being called "wiggle knees" as if he were a child.

Avery's mouth had gone dry, because the man standing in front of her was no child. He was devastatingly handsome in his blue dinner jacket and silver tie. The royal colors did wonderful things against his dark hair and olive skin. His deep brown eyes were full of amusement at Rosa and appreciation when he stared at Avery. He stared and stared as if drinking her in.

She suddenly felt like she was swimming in eggnog.

"I see Rosa has worked her magic once again."

Rosa twittered. "It was not difficult. She has a fine figure, *si?*"

Avery's cheeks positively burned. Her bare shoulders and collarbone suddenly felt very exposed, and she knew the fabric hugged her curves—even giving her a little boost thanks to the bone corset sewn between the lining and the satin.

"She is *bellissima.*" He held out his hand like a gallant knight in a fairy tale. "She must have dancing lessons, *si?*"

"*Si. Si.*" Rosa pushed them toward the door. "There is no time to waste. The ball is tomorrow night. You must teach her the saltarello. It's tradition."

He smiled widely. "That's one tradition I can get behind."

"Good. Now go!" She shoved them out the door and shut it in their faces.

Avery stared at it for a moment before turning to look at Matteo. "I've never been kicked out of a seamstress's shop before."

He grinned. "How about sneaking into a ballroom? Have you done that?"

Her eyes went big and her heart raced with excitement. "No."

He laced their fingers together, and they sprinted off down the hall. Her bare feet didn't make a sound on the marble floors, and his dress shoes were made from expensive leather that whispered of his presence. No wonder he'd been able to sneak into the shop without her noticing.

Not even her dress made noise—which was a testament to the quality of fabric, because her prom dress had been obscenely loud.

They raced past sculptures and paintings, turning corners and dodging lighted pathways until they came upon the grand doorway. Her heart pounded in her chest, though she was hard pressed to tell if it was because Matteo held her hand or because they ran with such abandon through a castle like two lovers in a Shakespeare play.

Matteo put his ear against the ballroom double door as if listening for sounds on the other side. She leaned against it too, her face only inches from his. From here, she could see that he'd shaved for the evening, and her palm itched to cup his cheek. He smelled heavenly, a dark, woodsy scent coupled with a sharp aftershave and something that was just him.

"The door is made of two-inch walnut. A marching band could be in that room and we wouldn't know it." Still, she whispered in case there was someone on this side of the door, perhaps in an adjoining hallway, who would bust them.

"How do you know that?"

She rolled her eyes. "I took the tour, remember?" She pointed to the right and then crooked her finger for him to follow.

He balked in surprise but did as she requested, his fingers on her lower back so he didn't lose her in the dark.

She got to the corner and felt around for the small doorknob. "Aha." She twisted and then fell into the ballroom as the door sprang open and practically pulled her off her feet.

Matteo reached out and caught her around the middle.

She breathed heavily. "You saved my dress."

He chuckled. "I think I saved you."

"That too. But I would have felt horrible if I'd ripped a seam." She searched his face lit by the moonlight through the small windows. Where the dining room was bathed in natural light, the ballroom was dark and intimate even with such grand space.

He set her back on her feet, the floor cold against her skin. She shivered, not just because her toes protested, but because her whole body missed having him close.

Matteo went to the wall, running his hand along it, probably looking for a light switch. "Rosa was quite taken with you. I do not think she would mind so much if she had to see you again to repair the dress."

Thinking of the way they'd been pushed out of her studio, Avery laughed. "I have a feeling that I could get away with murder in this castle, as long as I was with you."

"Well, not murder." He clicked something, and the wall sconces lit. They burned as low as candles and didn't do much good, except they cast enough light that she was able to see the decorated Christmas trees that stood in groups along the walls and in the corners. The bar was set up along one side, and the refreshment tables were next to it. They were bare as bones, but she could practically smell the sugar and Isola cheeses she'd come to love. Boughs of holly draped across the walls, wrapped in navy and silver ribbon.

Avery spun in a slow circle, taking in the room and the magical feeling of standing in a beautiful dress with a handsome man waiting to ask her to dance. As closely as she admired the room, when she met his gaze, she found Matteo was admiring her just as much. Blushing, she glanced down at the floor, which gleamed.

Matteo cleared his throat. "Have you had dance lessons before?"

She scoffed. "I was more of a softball girl."

His forehead wrinkled. "Well, then, we have much to do." He extended his hand with the other tucked behind his back. "The saltarello is a traditional dance."

She slipped her hand into his in a way that was both foreign and totally natural.

He used his thumb to capture her fingers. "Stand as I do, with your arm out to the side."

She turned so they faced the same direction,

lifting her chest and fixing her posture to match his.

He twisted his lips in concentration. "You know how a song has a chorus?"

"Yes."

"This dance has a step that's repeated like a chorus. It's right step, left step, right hop. And then you step backward and hop again."

He did the steps, and she followed, feeling ridiculously light and graceful. It helped that he was so confident in his movements. "When did you first learn to dance?" she asked.

"At five."

She missed a hop. He kept going, and she got back into the rhythm. "Did you like it?"

He bobbed his head side to side. "It was a chance to move about in an otherwise boring school day, so yes. Although it was just my brother and me for years. They didn't let us practice with actual girls until we were in our preteens and able to participate in a ball. I think you've got it." He grinned, and she did too. The step wasn't that hard.

"What's next?"

"We drop hands and I twirl."

She snorted a laugh as he put one hand over

his head and one around his front and did a hop-step into a twirl.

"What is funny?"

"I've never seen a grown man twirl before."

He scowled. "Men twirl. The king twirls in this dance, for heaven's sake."

"You're cute when you're defending your man card." She took his hand and started them in the basic step again, encouraging him to continue the lesson while they talked.

"You're cute in your bare feet." He twirled and then nodded for her to do the same.

She took her hop-step twirl and grinned in triumph. "Thankfully, you're a good dancer and haven't stepped on my feet—yet."

"Yet?" He put one hand on her side and lifted the other in an arc above his head. She copied his stance, and then he hop-stepped them in a circle. Their gazes met, and he held her there. She couldn't look away from the intensity, happiness, and attraction pouring out of him. It was as if she were looking right into his soul.

"There's always a first time," she rasped.

His gaze dipped to her lips. "What about a second?"

She instantly flashed to the moment in the

garden when he'd kissed her. "I'm a fan of second times."

His arm at her side slipped behind her and slowly drew her closer to him. Even with the layers of clothing, she could feel the warmth of his body and wondered what it would be like to have someone like him to lean on and lean into on a regular basis.

No, not someone like him. *Him.* She wanted to be with him.

His hand cupped her cheek, and his mouth lowered to hover above hers.

She grabbed his hand. "Matteo," she whispered, hardly able to get words past the attraction thudding in her chest. Fear of having to walk away when the blizzard stopped had her gripping his jacket. "Is this for real?"

He paused. Running his fingers over her cheek, he leaned in and nuzzled her neck. "You are the most real thing in my life."

Heady sensations at his touch threatened to overtake her. "What about after Christmas?"

He pulled back, tracing his eyes over her face and then looking her in the eye. "I'm working on that, *cuore mio.* I promise to do all that I can so that I will be free …" He took her hand in his and kissed her fingers. "... to explore a future with you."

Her mind spun as she worked to grab on to what he was saying, even as her body seemed to float above the floor. Were her feet even on the ground? "You aren't free now?"

He shook his head slightly. "Tradition and expectations hang over my head but not my heart. My heart is right here." He touched just below the hollow of her throat. "With you."

Overcome by the beauty of his words, she closed her eyes and rested her forehead against his chin. "Is this crazy? Are we? We hardly know one another, but I feel as if I've found a missing piece to my life." She bit her lip, worried that she'd said too much, moved too fast, or assumed he felt things he didn't. But he was the one speaking of hearts and holding her as if she were a masterpiece. How was she supposed to withstand his charms when completely surrounded by them?

"It is not crazy." He hooked a finger under her chin and brought her eyes up to meet his once again. How she loved their warmth! "These things are not planned by us—but they are planned by angels."

Tears stung, built on her lashes, and then spilled over.

"What is it, *cuore mio*?" He brushed the moisture away with his thumbs.

"Rosa said she felt my parents were in the castle with me. That they were watching out for me and wanted to bring me love." She hiccupped and then laughed at herself. She always did that when she cried.

"Then I must thank them." He kissed her cheek, moving slowly and with great care. His breath was warm on her skin, like a caress. She shivered again, this time from the delicious feelings Matteo lit on fire with his touch.

His hands moved across the sides of her dress and to the back, where he pressed his hands flat and began to sway them back and forth. She moved with him, not needing music to dance. Her arms wound around his neck, and she buried her fingers in the soft hair at the base of his skull. He moaned softly, the hum running through his chest and into hers. She trembled at the sensation, never having been this close or this in tune with a man. Never having danced with a real man before, one who knew how to lead her body in such a way that she was carried away.

He kissed her cheek once more before

brushing his lips across hers. The touch seared her with heat; at the same time, it created a hunger inside of her for more. She moaned, and he responded by tipping her head and deepening the kiss.

There was no urgency in his movements, but a sure confidence that had her gasping for breath. He pulled back, swallowed, and breathed. His forehead came to rest against hers, and she couldn't stop the smile that lifted her cheeks.

"Do you feel this?" He took her hand and laid it over his chest. His heart beat fast, pounding against his ribs.

Avery gasped. "Did I do that?" She stood in awe that she'd had that effect on such a strong, devastatingly handsome man.

He nodded.

Her smile widened. "Not too shabby for a Midwest girl." She giggled, and Matteo chuckled in response.

"Stay," he whispered. "Stay and dance with me." He began to sway again.

Avery tucked her head between his shoulder and his chin, loving how perfectly she fit in that space, like it had been carved just for her. "I'll stay." It wasn't an invitation to remain in Isola for life, but he'd explained that there were things in their way. She could give him time to work through those.

Never mind that she had a job waiting for her and an apartment to clean out. It all seemed a world away at the moment. The only thing that really mattered was the sense that she'd found a place that felt like home. Being in Matteo's arms was everything she'd been missing in her life.

CHAPTER 19

MATTEO

Matteo hummed to himself as he made his way back to his wing of the castle. The last kiss good night to Avery had been bittersweet. What he wouldn't give to wrap her up at night and hold her close. Alas, even if he was willing to overthrow hundreds of years of Christmas Eve tradition, he could not soil her reputation. He was a gentleman, after all.

Which was nice to know. In all this thwarting authority, he'd started to wonder what kind of a man he was—if he was dishonorable or honorable. There were those who would think him a rebel or worse. But if he knew who he was, he could handle the bad press and the jilting comments whispered behind hands but loud enough that he could hear. Over time, opinions would change.

He opened the door to his rooms, thankful that he'd told Alfredo to take his leave after dinner. He hadn't intended to dance until the middle of the night and would have felt awful if the old man was kept waiting. Because he would have waited out of a sense of duty.

He smiled as he undid his tie and rolled it around his hand. The lamps in his receiving room were on. Thankful he could see his way around, he walked over to turn them off only to find his brother sleeping on his couch. That just wouldn't do. The future king would have a crick in his neck come morning. Although leaving him there would mean that whatever he'd come to discuss would also wait until morning.

Brotherly duty ruled out his desire to remain in the dark. He shook him. "Angelo."

Angelo slowly opened his eyes, blinking against the soft lamps as if they were the noonday sun. He glanced around as if just realizing that he'd fallen asleep while here. "Where have you been?"

Matteo threw his tie on the coffee table and

pulled a water bottle out of the small fridge that looked like a regular wall. Instead of going on the defensive, he asked, "Why are you hiding in my rooms? Did your wife kick you out?"

"No." Angelo scowled. "Though I'd rather be in her bed than on this couch." He rubbed his neck.

Curiosity burned a trail through Matteo's brain with questions. Was Angelo welcome there? Obviously, he had been at least once, but there were obligations the firstborn son had to fulfill. Had the two moved into a more domestic arrangement lately?

Matteo scrubbed his hand over his face in frustration. What was he, a gossiping old man? "*Buona notte*, Angelo. Sleep wherever you wish."

"*Aspettare*." He held up a hand to stop Matteo from leaving. "I came to speak with you."

The hairs on Matteo's neck stood up in warning. They'd done that since he was a child. Madre called it a gift of premonition. He'd never been so sure. He turned, folding his arms and planting his feet. "Then speak."

Angelo sighed. "You created quite the stir at dinner."

Dinner was ages ago—a whole different time.

He could now mark the events of his life as before loving Avery and after loving Avery. Tonight, while watching the moonlight play upon her bare shoulders, he'd fallen in love.

"Luciana's father pulled me aside and asked if he should prepare his estate for a wedding or not."

"What did you tell him?"

Angelo sighed. "That all would be revealed at the ball."

Matteo nodded. "Thank you." Angelo could have insisted that everything was in line, as it had always been, for Luciana to marry within a year. He could have spoken for Matteo and made things more difficult. But he'd been evasive. Probably because he didn't know what was going on in Matteo's head. Matteo had only figured it out himself a few hours ago. After dancing with Avery in an empty ballroom, he'd realized that all the princely things could be taken from his life, and as long as he had her, he would be happy.

Angelo got to his feet. "I am not here to lecture you on being a prince."

"That is refreshing," Matteo quipped.

Angelo sighed. "Why do you think it's easy for me to put aside my personal needs?"

"Because you are older and more responsible."

"No. It is because I love this people. I don't see a mass of strangers out there who wave as our motor carriage parades by. I love Luca and Alfredo, Rosa and Bentry and Bambiana. They are my family—our family."

Matteo slowly lowered his arms. "I love them too. But I also believe—no, I *know* that they love me and want my happiness. I think you underestimate them."

Angelo shook his head. "If you pursue this path, you will bring heartache to our entire family."

"Not if you stand with me." Matteo crossed the room and put his hand on his brother's shoulder. "With the support of the future king, our people would rally behind change. This is about more than just when and whom I marry. It's about broadening our leadership and inviting new ideas into our country."

Angelo patted Matteo's hand on his shoulder. "I cannot go against Padre. This path is one you must travel alone. I am sorry."

Matteo nodded mutely. What had he expected? Angelo was who he was—and at his core, he was a king. There was a sting, though, one that came because his brother did not stand beside him.

Matteo was still standing in that same spot as the door clicked shut behind Angelo.

He grabbed a pad of paper and a pen out of the side table and drew a line down the middle. "I am sure ..." he wrote on one side. Then he proceeded to write the things he knew without a doubt.

"I cannot marry Luciana." He'd known that truth even before Avery.

"I want Avery in my life." To marry? Eventually. Hopefully sooner rather than later. She'd made a comment tonight about them moving fast, and as much as he wanted to sweep her off her feet and make her his princess, he wanted her to be sure. She would have to move here. She would have to leave her old life behind. She would have to change so many things, give up so much, just because he was a prince.

Which he still needed to tell her.

"I love my family." He said the words as he wrote. They rang with as much truth as anything else he'd written. Despite their recent squabbles, he was loyal to them. He threw the pad and pen on the table without trying to fill in the other side of the sheet. What was the point when two of his top three truths contradicted the other?

He laid his hand over his eyes and did his best

to seek inspiration from a higher source. "If there is a way out of this, Father God, please reveal it to me."

His plea was met with nothing but the ticking of the grandfather clock in the hall.

CHAPTER 20

AVERY

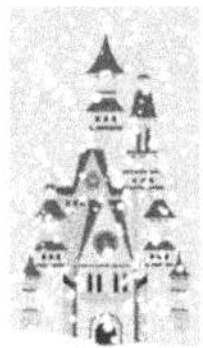

Avery hugged herself as soft snowflakes fell on her hat and piled on her shoulders. She should be cold, but snuggling up to Matteo in the back of a sleigh kept her plenty warm. Their driver, an older woman with round shoulders and a dark green coat and top hat, kept her eyes forward.

Matteo's face was hardly visible what with the thick scarf he'd wrapped around his neck. But his eyes were expressive enough. They spoke of kisses and promises and a night of dancing at the royal ball.

She still wanted to giggle at the whole idea that she would attend a ball. It was wonderfully ridiculous that her life had taken this turn. If someone had asked her at age eight what she thought her life would be like when she grew up, she would not have come anywhere close to sleeping in a castle—let alone leaving the country where she was born. Yet here she was, sitting next to a man she adored and delivering food to those in need.

And she loved him.

There was no denying it. She was in love with Matteo. How could she not be when he was everything she'd ever wanted and never hoped to find? He helped her be better, to see the world brighter, to open herself up to love once again. He was her match, her person.

Thank you, Mom and Dad, she silently whispered to the open sky, hoping her angel parents could hear her and know that she was happy. They could rest in peace because she'd found her place.

The sled stopped at a small home, the wreath sad and worn-looking. Matteo jumped out and offered his hand. She took it, stepping down carefully so she didn't slip. She'd almost fallen at their last stop, and Matteo had cautioned her about injuring her *twirling* foot.

"Real women twirl," she'd said with a wink.

He went to the smaller sled behind them and

retrieved a box. Inside were several bags of noodles, ravioli, tomato and alfredo sauces, fresh vegetables and fruits, the traditional fish, and a whole chicken along with a bouquet of fresh herbs from the greenhouse—fixings for a proper Christmas meal for the family who had applied for aid after a personal hardship. The forms with the addresses didn't say what the family was going through, but sometimes it was easy to spot.

Avery knocked on the door, since Matteo's hands were full, and stepped back. This was their last stop for the day. She was sad that their time together outside of the castle would be at an end, but there was so much to do to get ready for the ball that she was anxious to get back.

The door cracked open, no doubt to keep the warm air in the house, and a pair of light eyes stared up at them from a small child.

Matteo spoke rapidly in Italian, and the door soon opened, allowing them in. Avery hurried to shut out the wind. It wasn't blowing as hard as it had been. The weather reports were optimistic that they'd have clear skies on Christmas morning. It seemed the storm had almost blown itself out. She wasn't afraid of their travel restrictions lifting anymore. Matteo had calmed those fears with deep kisses and softly murmured promises.

The child replied. While Avery's Italian was good enough to get her through the streets, to a bathroom, and pick up a word here and there, she couldn't keep up with these two. Matteo pointed to her and the boy rushed her, throwing his arms around her middle and burying his face in her coat. "*Gratzie. Ti amo.*"

That much she understood. "I love you too." She hugged him back, and then he dropped his arms and went to inspect the box.

Matteo motioned for the door. "His *madre* will be back in a few minutes. We should be out of the area by then."

She hurried out, making sure the door shut tightly behind them. "I love this. Leaving the gifts when no one but the children are home. Where are all the adults, anyway?"

He glanced up that the gray sky. "Probably shopping. The weather has made it difficult for them to get out."

She helped him pull the blankets up over their knees. The large bricks Alfredo had placed under their feet were warm. She smiled. Such an old way of doing things, but it worked wonderfully. She tipped her head up and let the snow tickle her cheeks as it fell. "I wish every day could be like this."

"Snowy and cold?" Matteo poked her side, teasing.

"No!" She lightly elbowed him. "It's nice not to have to worry about work or rent or any of those things and to focus on Christmas." She lifted a shoulder. "Being here is like being outside of reality, and yet I've never felt more—" She stopped, afraid to say what was in her heart.

"What?" Matteo prodded.

She rolled her eyes. "What is it about you that makes me want to spill my guts?"

He made a face and leaned back. "What did you have for breakfast?"

She laughed. "That's not what that means. It means I tell you things I don't mean to, nor do I tell them to anyone else."

He settled himself back in his seat, his eyes wide like a child's waiting for their favorite movie to come on screen. "Speak."

She dropped her face in her hand. "I feel most like myself when I'm with you. There, are you happy?"

The heat that built in his eyes was unmistakable. He pulled his scarf down and claimed her mouth. The kiss was short and hot and left her puffing air like a dragon. "I am very happy, *signorina*."

"Me too." She snuggled deeper into the blanket and his side. She truly couldn't believe that this was her life. That she was riding in an open, horse-drawn sleigh with a man who she might really and truly love. Nothing could ruin this moment.

They hit a bump, and his jaw knocked her head. They both laughed, rubbing their sore spots.

"I'm sorry. But I think the horse threw a shoe." Their driver pulled the animal to a stop and then hopped down.

Avery grabbed the side of the sleigh and leaned out. The driver had lifted the horse's back foot. The hoof looked ragged and rough. "Is that normal?" She scooted back so Matteo could look.

He squinted. "No." With one leap, he was out of the sleigh and talking to the driver, who gestured wildly with her hands in return.

"No, no, no, no," she told him.

Matteo replied with, "*Si. Si. Si.*" Though he was good-natured about it while the woman was flushed and flustered. He made his way back to Avery and held out his hand. "It appears we're walking."

"To the castle?" Avery turned to look up, up, up the hill to where the castle spires loomed above the capital.

"I'm afraid so."

"Isn't there someone we can call?" She had her cell. They were barely going to be on time for her to get ready as it was; walking would put her behind schedule.

He shook his head. "They are preparing for the ball. We are short-staffed, and I don't want to pull someone away from their job because of this." He motioned to the horse, which had turned around to look at them as if waiting for her to get out so he could get on with his day.

She nodded, steeling herself against the long hike in the snow. "All right. It can't be worse than climbing the stairs to the top of the Vatican."

He chuckled. "I don't know if you just insulted Isola or the Vatican."

"Neither." She hopped out, landed solidly on both feet, and grinned. "It was a compliment."

"It didn't feel like a compliment." He took her gloved hand, and they started off down the road that would wind its way to the castle gate.

She laughed, her breath puffing out around her. "Come on. We have to hurry, or I won't have time to get ready for the ball."

Her dress was waiting in Rosa's studio. She'd returned it when she'd gathered her clothes. It didn't actually belong to her, and she felt strange taking it down to the servants' quarters—like she was bragging to the other girls or something. She didn't want to be *that* person.

The hike was at least three miles of switchbacks. She huffed but managed to keep pace. Whoever decided to put the castle on the hill must have had thighs of steel.

By the time they straggled up to the front doors, her hair hung in wet clumps and her nose was numb and runny. She hoped the contrast between what she looked like now and what she'd look like after primping for the ball would knock Matteo's socks off. Though she hated leaving this image in his head for even a couple hours.

The front doors to the castle were open as deliveries streamed in. Several of these cars and vans passed them on the road up but didn't stop. The royal ball was probably more important than two weary travelers on the eve of Christ's birth. She smiled, thinking of the comparison, and heard her mom say, "What would Jesus do?" in her head.

A maid in uniform rushed out to grab flowers

from the back of a van. She glanced their way and then dropped into a curtsy. *"Buon Natale, principe."*

Avery stopped and blinked. "My ears must be frozen. I thought she called you prince."

Matteo tugged her into the castle, the temperature rising dramatically due to the portable heaters set right inside the door. Her nose began to run in earnest now, and she sniffed several times, patting her pockets for a tissue she didn't think she had.

Matteo handed her a white cotton handkerchief with something embroidered on the corner.

"Thank you." She did her best to be dainty as she wiped her nose. People moved around them, and she worked to get out of the constant stream going in and out.

"Buon Natale," said a man in a white chef's coat. His face was red, as if he were embarrassed, and he half bowed as he passed.

That was so weird. Avery glanced around, noting that most of the people either ducked their heads or bowed slightly as they passed. "What's happening?"

Matteo took her arm and moved them off to the side. "I have to get ready."

"Principe Matteo," called a woman Avery's age

with jet-black hair, striking eyebrows, and a killer brown suit. She strode toward them with all the elegance of a queen.

Avery gave her nose one more swipe and wished her face wasn't flushed from the cold.

"*Principe*, I must speak with you in private." She didn't glance at Avery, though Avery was well aware that she was the one the woman wanted gone.

Matteo set his jaw. "Luciana, I have nothing to say to you."

Avery blinked several times. Knowing Matteo was on a first-name basis with this woman made her feel things—ugly green-colored things that brought out claws and bared teeth.

"*Principe, per favore*, we must speak before the announcement."

There was that word again. Avery shook her head as the translation came through. Prince. "Why does she keep calling you prince?" She waved her hand around. "Why are these people calling you prince?" She put some force into her words, because she was pretty sure she knew the answer, but she wasn't going to like it. Her brain didn't want to organize the puzzle pieces floating around. She fought against it but had to know. Because … because … because if Matteo was a prince, then that meant he was getting engaged tonight. Her hand flew to her lips—the very ones that had burned and tingled as his mouth covered hers.

The woman snapped her fingers as if Avery were a dog she was trying to get to pay attention. "Because he is Principe Matteo de la Luca." She then rattled off something in Italian that Avery didn't need translated to know was a derogatory comment.

Other dots connected. Avery's hands went to her stomach, which had suddenly dropped to the floor. "You're getting engaged tonight." She stepped back from him. "You're the prince that's getting engaged." Her eyes darted back and forth between the two of them. And she knew.

She knew this woman was supposed to be his princess.

"Avery, please understand." He reached for her arm, but she sidestepped his touch.

"No." Her eyes stung, and she hiccupped, tears threatening. "I thought this was more to you than a holiday tryst."

"It is," he insisted.

She clenched her fists. "Well, I'm not about to stick around as the prince's mistress."

"Avery!" His mouth fell open and his eyes filled with hurt. "Do you think so little of me?"

She pointed at Luciana, who stood with her arms folded, letting the drama play out and drinking it in like eggnog. "I don't know what to think. I know you lied." Her brain was all muddled. Like driving a dirt road in the spring, she couldn't get her mental tires to grip enough to propel her thoughts forward. "You said you were an advisor."

"As the second son, that is all I will ever be."

"But you are a prince?" She had to hear it from him. Had to give him the chance to make this right. Though she wasn't sure how that would ever be.

He swallowed. "Yes."

"See, that's kind of an important part of the conversation."

"Why?" His eyes pleaded with her to stop being angry, to just hold him close and love him forever.

But how could she do that when he was going to marry another woman? It just wasn't possible. "Because an advisor can quit, but a prince is—"

"A life sentence," he finished for her.

"No." She shook her finger at him, anger at being played the fool building inside of her. "You don't get to cry, 'Poor, poor me, I was born a prince.' Not to me. You have a family, Matteo. I would give everything I have and more to live in a place like this where you have dozens of people who love you. I have no one."

"Avery." He whispered her name.

She took a step backward. "At least for a time, I had you." She wouldn't regret loving him. No. It was that love that had repaired her broken heart. For that, she'd always be grateful. But his lie? That was pain—different from what she'd felt when her parents had died but no less intense.

Needing to get out of there before she burst into ugly tears and ruined the carpet, she turned and ran. He wouldn't follow her into the servants' quarters. Hadn't ever. She'd thought he was being a gentleman, but now she wondered if there was a rule about the prince going "below stairs" or whatever they called it in Isola.

She made it through the door and collapsed against it, sobbing. Brandy found her there a while later, lifted her to standing, and walked her to their shared room. The whole time, all she could do was cry about the family she thought she'd found and now lost.

Then there was man who had captured her

heart completely. She hadn't even known how deeply she loved him until she couldn't have him.

No woman should lose two families in a lifetime. That was too much.

But to lose Matteo? That was what brought her to her knees.

CHAPTER 21

MATTEO

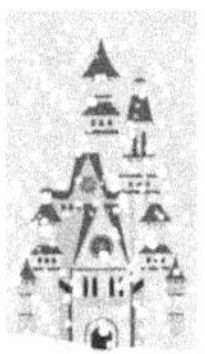

Matteo stared after Avery as she ran though the throngs. Servers, delivery personnel, and maids watched him out of the corner of their eyes, trying not to look like they were listening intently as his heart crumbled. He was sure there were cracking noises as it dried up and died.

"What did you want, Luciana?" It took every ounce of training Alfredo had put him through over the last 27 years to keep from screaming at her.

"I was actually going to ask you about the rumors floating about the castle that there was a mystery woman in your life." She smirked. "But I think there's no reason for concern."

He gritted his teeth. "Luciana, the very fact that you view me as a prize instead of a person is the reason that I will not announce an engagement to you tonight."

Her mouth fell open and her usual polish slipped, revealing the ugly woman hiding behind the makeup and designer suits. "You cannot do this to me, Matteo. I've been groomed my whole life to be a princess."

"You'll just have to look elsewhere. Catalonia has several princes of marrying age—even the one in line for the crown."

Her eyes actually sparkled, and his stomach soured. "Perhaps you could provide an introduction, for old time's sake."

He managed to keep his face passive even as he mentally gagged. "*Si*. They will be at the ball tonight." And after he introduced them, he would pull the prince aside and give him fair warning. After all, he couldn't afford to ruin Isola's relationship with the country that grew rare oranges. They had a nice thing going between their annual crop and Isola's bees.

She clapped her hands. "I'm going to get changed and talk to Padre. He'll be so excited."

"*Si. Si,*" Matteo said absently. At least one of them was happy about this. He was slowly drowning as the realization of what Avery had said sank in.

If it had been anyone else, the words would not have hit him with such force. But she was a woman without a family—and she envied his. He staggered to a chaise and fell into the soft fabric, worn over time by hundreds of women sitting here to remove their boots and put on their house shoes. His own grandmother and great-grandmother had sat here. Everywhere around him, there were pieces of his family. He'd always thought it was suffocating, but Avery saw it all as a comfort. Had he been looking at it wrong?

His ancestors had made sacrifices and swallowed pride and been women the world admired. They'd borne children and raised them to be full of honor and to have a love for Isola that was greater than themselves.

Alfredo rushed in, glancing around the entry way as if looking for a lost cat. When his eyes landed on Matteo, he made a beeline for him. "Principe, *per favore*, you must get dressed."

Matteo rolled his head to take in the man. He wore his usual stuffy suit and starched collar. "Are you comfortable?"

"*Scusi?*"

"Do you like wearing those clothes? Don't you ever want to wear sweatpants to work?"

Alfredo placed the back of his hand on Matteo's forehead. "Are you ill?"

Matteo let him check his temperature. "I mean it. Is there something you'd rather do than hang out here every day, waiting for me to need guidance and a change of clothing?"

Alfredo's hand dropped. His eyes were sad.

Matteo repented. "I didn't mean to insult you. I just meant, do you ever wonder if there's more life out there?" He pointed to the open door. The number of people coming in and out had thinned as preparations were taken care of.

Alfredo brushed off the seat and sat next to him. "I used to think that."

"Really? When?"

"When I was a little older than you." He smiled fondly at the memories. "I was a feisty young apprentice to my father, who looked after your father. I thought the castle walls were stifling."

He could relate. "What changed?"

Alfredo tugged at his jacket. "You were born." He continued to stare at the floor as if the truth were too honest to look at. "This child appeared. A second son of a king. And I saw a chance to make a difference in the world. He who influences a prince influences the world—my father used to say that."

Matteo shrank into the corner. "You got the wrong son."

"I don't think so." Alfredo looked at him then. "I see a man who thinks for himself and challenges those around him to do the same. That was not an accident."

Matteo looked, really looked at Alfredo. Memories popped into his head. Like the day he'd asked his tutor to teach him how to build a bottle rocket like the one he'd seen online. At first the man had refused, but Matteo had explained that learning the science behind explosions was a sound study for a prince. They'd spent that spring blowing things up on the beach and making fireworks for his birthday party. His mother still broke into a sweat whenever they had firework displays, despite the fact that Matteo made it out of the class with all his fingers—and eyebrows—still attached.

He never would have pushed to learn such a thing if Alfredo hadn't told him that a man must follow his interests because God put them there for a reason.

"I still don't know why I need to know how to

blow something up." Matteo smiled sadly at his longtime supporter.

"Because the knowledge gave you confidence when you needed it."

His frank answer both surprised and pleased Matteo. He had struggled that year. His arms and feet had been too long, and he'd had acne. Princes weren't supposed to have acne. Angelo never had acne.

Humbled that Alfredo had really seen him, he stuck out his hand. "I don't know what I would have done without you."

Alfredo looked at it before taking it. "It has been my honor, *principe*."

Matteo sighed. "I have made a mess of things now. Avery found out I'm a prince, and she doesn't want to have anything to do with me. I pushed Luciana off on Catalonia's heir—I'm sure that one will come back to bite me. And Padre hasn't spoken to me in days."

Alfredo leaned his head back against the wall. "That is all true. Though I did not know about Luciana."

He could care less, except he liked Prince Tolomeo. "How do I fix this?"

Alfredo huffed a breath. "Which one is most important?"

Without having to think about it, Matteo replied. "Avery. I want her in my life in every way."

"Are you willing to marry her?"

He smiled. "As the Americans say, ready, willing and able."

"Then you should go to the ball and make your intentions known to the world."

Matteo frowned. "Shouldn't I make them known to Avery?"

"Avery will be at the ball." Alfredo rolled one hand over the other.

"I don't think so."

Alfredo patted him on the shoulder. "Do not underestimate me. I will ensure she is there. And you must make a grand gesture." Alfredo shook his head as if Matteo had tied his tie backward. "You have messed up this much." He held his hands out about shoulder width apart. "Therefore, you must repent this big." He widened them to double the original size. "That is how you apologize properly to a woman."

Matteo grinned. "Wise words from a man who has never been married."

"Married? No. In love? Yes."

Matteo about fell off his seat. "You?"

Alfredo laughed. "Do you think you are the

only reason I stayed in the castle?" He pushed to his feet and tucked his hands behind his back. "Come, we must get you ready to make a fool of yourself for a woman."

"But—" Matteo jumped to his feet, eagerly dogging his steward's steps. "Who is she?"

Alfredo laughed but kept his mouth shut. Matteo swore he would figure out this mystery, *after* he won the fair Avery's heart and hand.

CHAPTER 22

AVERY

The world was one big blur. Seriously. Avery couldn't see a thing through the tears that wouldn't stop coming. A tissue found its way into her hand, and she used it to wipe her sore nose. It hurt from being blown a hundred times in the last hour.

"He's getting engaged," Brandy said for what must have been the thirteenth time. Avery had cried against the door, lost in her own grief and feelings of being stupid. How had she not known he was the prince?

Well, because she hadn't expected royalty to pay any attention to her, and so she hadn't worried about them. Why would the prince look twice at a Midwest girl like her who'd grown up getting average grades and playing softball? She wasn't anything special enough to draw a prince's eye.

Brandy was in as much shock as she was. She'd found Avery, hauled her back to their room, and let the story spill out like M&M's through a rip in the bag: messy, loud, and unpredictable.

"When I told you to go for it and have fun, I didn't know." Brandy's face was all *sorry* and *I should have known better.*

Avery leaned her head on her friend's shoulder. They sat side by side on the bed with their backs to the wall. "I know. Who would have known?"

"Sabrina, I guess." Brandy pulled out another tissue and handed it over. At this rate, Avery would go through the whole box. Darn it all, she felt bad about costing Matteo's family more money. "But it's not like Isola royalty are big on the internet. I had to search to find the pictures I did."

Avery averted her eyes as Brandy pulled her phone up. Her first step as best friend had been to verify Matteo's identity. Gah! He looked so good on a horse. Driving a convertible. Cutting the ribbon at a business opening. She couldn't stand to see his image on screen when there were so many others burned into her memory. And she'd lamented deleting those family pictures from her phone when all she had to do was go online to print out an 8x10 glossy of the prince.

There was a knock at the door, and it swung open, revealing Stacy and Tina. They wore black pants and black button-up shirts, their hair in ponytails. "We stopped by to see your dress …" Stacy trailed off as her eyes swept over the tissues and general sense of heartbreak in the room. "What happened?"

"Ummm." Brandy stalled, waiting for Avery to take the lead.

"I fell for a man who is not available." Avery buried her face in the tissue.

Tina gasped. "He's married!" Her hands splayed across her chest.

"No!" Brandy snapped. "He's getting engaged tonight."

Both women paused. "Like the prince?" Tina asked.

"*Exactly* like the prince." Brandy's emphasis on the first word told the whole story.

"Ooooooh." Stacy tucked one foot under her as she sat on the end of the bed. "Is he in love with this woman?"

"What does it matter?" Avery plucked at the

quilt. "I can't go to the ball and watch him propose to someone else. I just can't."

"Of course not." Tina gave Stacy a back-off look.

There was an awkward pause where everyone wanted to ask her questions and she wouldn't make eye contact to give them permission.

A rustling in the hallway had them all turning as Sabrina burst into the room with Rosa and the midnight-blue dress. Avery's tiny space was much too crowded. She just wanted to be alone to drown in her own tears and hiccup until her stomach was sore.

Avery pulled her knees up on the bed and pressed herself against the wall. Seeing the dress flooded her with the feeling of being in Matteo's arms and made her ache with longing.

Sabrina looked over the group. "What are you three doing here?"

"Consoling our friend." Brandy folded her arms.

Stacy and Tina nodded.

"You will be late, and it will reflect badly on me." Sabrina began making shooing motions and stepping closer. She even went so far as to poke Stacy to get her going. "Do not make me look bad in front of my family. You go to the kitchens and do your job."

The girls headed for the door. Brandy stopped to look over her shoulder. "Should I stay?"

"No!" Sabrina shoved her out. "I will take care of her." She shut the door and brushed off her hands.

Rosa grinned. "Just like your madre." She patted Sabrina's cheek fondly. "She is bossy too."

Sabrina laughed lightly. "*Gratzie*." She turned on Avery, and her lightness morphed into an I'm-in-chargeness. "Now, why are you sitting there with puffy eyes and a red nose when you are expected at the ball?" She shoved her hands under Avery's behind and threw her off the bed.

Avery stumbled, using the opposite wall to keep from falling. "Sabrina. I can't go to the ball. Matteo is proposing to someone tonight."

"Yes, and if we get you dressed, it could be you."

She stared at the tour guide, her mouth agape. "Wha-a-wha?"

Rosa giggled behind her hand like a schoolgirl. "I said the same thing when my husband proposed to me." Her eyes danced with mirth. "Did you know that there are men all over the country who have waited to propose to their loves until tonight, because it's good luck to propose on the same night as a royal?"

"Really?" It sounded crazy, but with all the traditional ways of Isola, it also made sense.

"My husband, may he have peace with God, couldn't wait. Neither could I." She winked. Then she turned to hang the dress over the hinge on the door. It was only then that Avery saw the large bag hanging over her shoulder. Rosa reached in and pulled out a makeup bag. "Fetch a cold cloth for her eyes," she told Sabrina, who ducked out to do as she was told.

Rosa watched her leave out of the corner of her eye. "I have it on good information that the prince sent Luciana packing. He wants nothing to do with her, because he has fallen in love with you." She pulled a brush out of the bag and turned Avery around so she could get the tangles out of her hair. It was slightly damp from her hike in the snow, and Rosa wasn't shy about tugging.

Avery sniffed and then hiccupped. "What am I supposed to do? Crash the royal ball and hope he's not mad at me?"

"Oh, *bambina,* he will not be angry with you."

"But I told him I couldn't see him again. That I didn't want to."

"You are a passionate woman, *si*. Isola men would not have their woman any other way."

Avery shook her head. "You're trying to talk me into chasing after him."

"No!" Rosa smacked her head with the brush.

"Ow!" Avery ducked and scooted out of the way, rubbing her noggin. "That hurt."

"You do not chase the man." She shook the brush her direction. "He will chase you, or you will walk out of the ball with your head held high."

"Okay, okay." Avery held up her hands, ready to grab for the brush if it came her way again.

Sabrina reappeared with a white washcloth. "Here, put this on your eyes." She took the brush from Rosa, and Avery dared to cover her face.

Sabrina brushed and then began separating sections, creating an intricate updo that would show off Avery's slender neck.

Avery did as they asked and told. She allowed them to dress her up like a doll, exclaiming over every step as if they were masters at the art of creating a princess. But inside, she knew that things weren't going to work out as Rosa and Sabrina predicted. She'd go to the ball, for them. Because Rosa's work on the dress was spectacular and a kindness she didn't have to bestow on the woman living in the servant quarters. She'd added silver beads in the shape of snowflakes that flurried across the bodice. It was stunning.

Avery didn't want to embarrass Sabrina in front of her family either. She'd stick to the walls, maybe taste some punch, and then slip away to her room to pack. As soon as the airport opened up, she'd get a flight—it would be easier to change her ticket if she flew alone.

CHAPTER 23

MATTEO

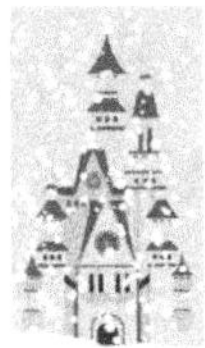

Matteo lined up with his family for the royal procession into the ball. His parents were first, then Angelo and Aria. Next, he would walk alone with his sisters trailing behind him. He glanced back to see them looking much older than their young lives should allow. He jerked his head for them to join him and held out his arms. Each sister took one, beaming up at him.

Angelo glanced back and glared. They always entered the same way as every royal family had since the beginning of the Christmas Eve balls—married couples together, singles alone. Well, this was one change Matteo wasn't going to ask permission to make. He wanted to enter with

Avery, but that wasn't a possibility. He smirked at Angelo as the live band began the Isola de la Familia anthem.

Alfredo held the door that went from the family's space to the ballroom. Matteo gave him a pleading look, begging for information about Avery. Had she left the castle? Was she coming? Alfredo kept a stoic face, but at the last second, he winked.

Matteo burst into a grin. The moment he entered the ballroom, he looked for Avery. The royal family was announced, the man stumbling over himself to get out Carlotta and Emmilia's names as they were aligned with Matteo instead of following a few feet behind.

Padre had to have noticed, but like the king he was, he didn't pause in his parade to the middle of the dance floor, where he took Madre in his arms for the opening dance. Angelo and Aria were ready. The girls looked up at him, confused. They normally stood on the sidelines, as they weren't considered old enough to take a dance partner yet. It was a shame, considering how much time they spent in lessons. Matteo bowed and offered each of them one hand. The accepted with smiles and grace.

Padre ignored him, probably thinking this was

one of his pranks or a purposeful way to act out. It wasn't. He loved his sisters and wanted to help them enjoy the ball. The music started, and the three of them made a perfect box step. Their smiles were so big, the pain in his heart lessened ever so slightly. After several more beats, the king motioned for others to join in, and dancing erupted around them.

Matteo used the dance to scan the crowd. He was tall enough to see over many, but he didn't spotted Avery. He tried not to worry, tried to have faith in Alfredo and his prediction that all would be well, but he felt as though he were standing on a cliff and a stiff breeze would send him over the edge.

When the song ended, he bowed to his sisters. "I have forever claimed a place in your history as the first man to dance with you at a ball."

They grinned back at him and then tugged him down to kiss his cheek.

He scowled. "Do not kiss every man you dance with, *si?*"

They giggled. "*Si.*"

The music for the next song started. Even though they were in the middle of the dance floor, no one was upset that they didn't dance as the next song began.

The girls laughed at his theatrics and proclamation.

Madre came alongside him. "That was very sweet of you, Matteo. Ladies, there are sweets you must sample tonight." She nodded toward the buffet tables, for a queen never points in public.

The girls linked arms and headed that way. *Bambiana,* in the traditional nanny uniform of a navy-blue knee-length dress and apron, followed.

Madre turned so she could stand next to Matteo and take in the room. "I heard a rumor that Luciana has set her sights on becoming a queen."

Matteo nodded. "I felt as though she wanted to rule me. I merely mentioned that running a country may be more of a challenge."

Madre chuckled. "I highly doubt that."

Matteo smiled at her.

"And what of your American princess?"

He rubbed his lips together. "I'm to make a grand gesture. *If* she comes."

"And if she doesn't?"

"I'll probably alienate Padre, upset the whole country, and then chase after her."

Madre's eyes softened. "Good."

Matteo took comfort in her approval.

The second song ended, and the royal

announcer banged his staff on the wood floor three times. Matteo and Madre moved closer to the stage. They would have to join Padre at some point in his toast, though they weren't to ascend the steps until he beckoned to them. Symbolic of the fact that he bore the weight of the kingdom on his shoulders. "The king of Isola de la Familia, Roberto de Luca."

Polite clapping filled the hall as Padre took his place on the stage. He held up a cup. Servers flooded the room, bearing trays of warm cider in small glasses with gold rims.

"This year, the people of Isola have been blessed with abundant crops and vats of honey. Our bees have visited almost every prospering nation and helped provide food for the human family." He glanced down at his cup and then back up. "Family is important to our people—it's important to me."

He motioned for all of them to come up. Madre went first, holding up her dress so as not to trip over it. Angelo and Aria went to Padre's right, standing a step below. Matteo was one step below them, and the girls were in front on his level.

"Each year, as we begin the Christmas celebrations, I think of what my life would be like without my family, and it seems bleak, empty, and so very quiet." He made a show of glancing at his two daughters, which earned him a laugh from the crowd. "This year is my son Matteo's twenty-seventh Christmas Eve."

An excited ripple went through the crowd. To witness the engagement of an Isoladian prince was something to tell your grandchildren about. Cell phones and cameras were banned, but the official photographers clicked away, capturing this moment for history.

Matteo's stomach churned. Avery was nowhere in sight. He searched for her beautiful face. He'd prayed she would be there. He looked for Alfredo, barely able to hear Padre's words over the rising thump-thump panic in his veins.

"It is tradition for a prince to choose his bride on this night," continued Padre.

Alfredo stepped in from the family's door and lifted his hands.

Matteo dropped his chin to his chest. She wasn't coming.

"But, upon reflection of my heart, I have decided to abolish this tradition."

A collective gasp sounded. Matteo's head snapped up. As it did, he caught a flutter of silver on blue, and his eye was drawn to the far wall, in the shadow of a Christmas tree, where Avery stared as if drinking in every bit of him.

"Padre." Matteo held out a hand for him to stop his pronouncement. He then took a step up and turned to face his father and his king. "What are you doing?"

Padre seemed to soften. "As your madre so eloquently pointed out earlier this evening, we are not *Isola de la Tradizione*. We are *Isola de la Familia*. You are my son." His voice became gruff, and he cleared his throat. "*Familia* will rule in my household."

Matteo surged up and planted a kiss on his madre's cheek. "Have I ever told you how intelligent you are?"

She kissed his cheek in return, squeezing his shoulders. "Be bold."

He turned to Padre and put out his hand. Padre looked at it for a moment, and then reached out and gave him a solid hug.

Humbled by the show of support and love in front of their whole country, Matteo could easily show his padre the respect due to his king. "If it pleases you, I would like to ask Avery Rossi of America to be my bride on this, my twenty-seventh Christmas Eve." He didn't speak loudly, but those closest to the raised platform heard and began to whisper the information to those behind them. The whole room was a buzz with the words *American* and *Avery*.

Padre swallowed as if choking down a hundred years of expectations. "So be it."

Matteo spun, his eyes landing on the shadow next to the Christmas tree. When he spoke, he raised his voice to be heard in every corner of the large room. "Amici y familia ..." He began walking down the steps and across the room. Avery looked in every direction, possibly trying to find a way out. He hoped she didn't run, but if she did, he would chase her. "Our country is small in size, but we are large in tradition. We hold fast to the old ways because they have proven themselves over time."

The crowd parted in front of him, curious looks abounding.

"But we are entering a new age." He stopped in front of Avery. She was even more stunning than last night. Her hair was up in a traditional Isoladian braid, and her makeup was flawless. He just stared, forgetting his speech and his grand gesture and all of Alfredo's advice. "You are stealing my breath away," he barely managed to whisper.

She blushed and ducked her head.

The break in eye contact allowed his brain to turn back on. Where was he? Oh! "It will take strong families to guide us through the coming years."

He held his hand out to her, and she hesitated, finally slipping her fingers into place. His whole soul expanded with relief at her touch. She was here, for him, and he would forever be hers.

"I am grateful to the king for his graciousness and for his fatherly love." He turned so he stood next to Avery, holding their hands up between them as if they were going to start a dance. In this way, he led her back to the stage, where he stopped on the lower level.

Avery was not a royal. She could not ascend the steps—not yet, anyway.

"However, I have found a woman who not only holds my heart, but who values family more than anyone I know. She will make an excellent Isoladian."

Avery's hand shook in his. He didn't want to let her go, but he had to get the ring out of his pocket. He fumbled, making his grand gesture slightly less grand. Avery's eyes sparkled, and he knew that she knew he was nervous. Not because he stood in front of over a hundred guests, declaring his love, but because he truly didn't know if she would say yes.

He reached for her hand and lowered himself to one knee. "Avery Rossi, you have shown me courage and kindness, grace and adventure, and you have stolen all my love. Will you marry me, *cuore mio?*"

The crowd oohed and aahed as he held up his great-grandmother's sapphire engagement ring.

Avery's eyes glistened as she nodded. Her lips pressed tightly together as if she were trying to hold back a happy sob. He surged to his feet, picking her up in the process, and swung her around as the whole room applauded. Trumpets erupted with joyful noise.

He stopped and placed her on her feet and then slipped the ring on her finger. It fit perfectly. Avery sighed happily and leaned against him.

He placed his hands on her cheeks and kissed her softly. "I am sorry I didn't tell you I was a prince."

She met his gaze. "I'm sorry I doubted you."

"Well!" Padre called from the top step. "This calls for a celebration. Maestro." He waved his arm, and the band began to play the traditional saltarello. Couples formed lines.

Avery's face lit up. "I know this one."

Matteo laughed. "Come. Dance with me, *cuore mio.*"

"Are you happy?" Avery asked low. "I mean, you didn't propose to me because you had to, did you?"

He chuckled and brought her hand to his lips so he could kiss her fingers. "Actually, I did."

Her face fell.

"But only because my life would be nothing without you. So you see, I had to propose."

She slugged him in the arm, making him laugh.

"Are you happy?" he asked her just before executing a perfect twirl.

She grinned. "What woman wouldn't be happy with a man who twirls?"

He laughed loudly, drawing the attention of those around them. "Real men twirl."

"So I've been told."

He stopped dancing and pulled her close, needing to kiss her right then and there. When he pulled back, aware that he was causing a scene, she smiled up at him shyly.

"We are going to have beautiful babies." He brushed a finger over her cheek.

"Matteo!" she scolded, and she looked around to see who had overheard.

He grinned, feeling light and happy and so full he might burst. The Christmas he'd dreaded for years had turned out to be his best one. He'd found the love of his life and had the freedom to love her forevermore.

"Buon Natale," he whispered into her hair.

She tipped her head up and smiled at him. "Merry Christmas."

CHAPTER 24

AVERY

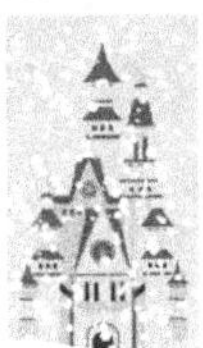

Avery stretched out in the soft sheets and moaned. Her legs were sore from dancing the night away. She and Matteo couldn't get enough of being in one another's arms. Even after the band packed up and the staff cleared the buffet tables and all the lights except for the ones on the trees were turned out, they swayed to the song of their love.

She smiled. That was what Matteo had called it: the song of their love.

He was so romantic.

She pulled her hand up in front of her face and opened her eyes, wanting the first thing she saw to be the ring he had placed on her finger.

It. Was. Stunning. And apparently a priceless heirloom to boot.

She lowered her hand and looked around the room. After the ball, Matteo had walked her to his old bedroom, part of his parents' suite, gave her a long kiss good night, and said she was to make herself welcome.

She'd barely dared touch anything, but she was tired. And the bed was inviting. A pair of pajamas was laid out on the coverlet. Her pajamas. And her backpack leaned against the dresser. Which meant Brandy was in on this—and maybe Alfredo. She couldn't wait to catch up with her friends.

The door flew open and Carlotta and Emmilia flew in, their bare feet pounding on the wood floors. *"Buon Natale!"*

She pulled herself up as they landed on the bed, bouncing on their knees. *"Buon Natale,"* she replied happily. She planned to work on her Italian so she could understand all the sweet words Matteo whispered—it was the highest form of motivation, as far as she was concerned.

"Babbo Natale came last night. There are piles of presents under the tree." Emmilia made fists and pressed them over her mouth as if she might just burst open with excitement.

"Wonderful. You must have been good this year."

Carlotta climbed up next to her and snuggled into her side. "What did you do on Christmas morning when you were little?"

Taken off guard by the question, Avery had to think for a moment. "Well, my dad would make cinnamon pancakes and my mom made hot chocolate. We'd eat and open presents and then play games together."

"Sounds wonderful," Matteo's deep voice sounded at the door. He looked amazing in jeans and a Henley, his hair still wet from a shower.

Avery wanted to hide under the covers. She had bedhead and a layer of mascara under her eyes.

Matteo didn't seem to mind, as he couldn't take his eyes off her. "I thought I heard Padre walking in his room."

The girls exchanged a look and took off out of the room.

Matteo laughed. "We can't open gifts until everyone wakes up," he explained.

Avery glanced down.

"Everyone includes you now, *cuore mio*." He sat on the edge of her bed. "Do you think you will mind moving here? We have not spoken of this, and I do not want to assume it will be the case. But I feel as though I can make a difference for my people, and I would like to try."

"I would love to live here. When we are together, I am home." She slowly lifted her eyes. "I want to thank you."

"There is no need to thank me." He sat on the edge of the bed and kissed her forehead.

She shook her head slightly. "There is. I thought I would spend this Christmas alone. And maybe many more after that before I—" Her voice caught.

"Ah, *cuore mio,* you will never be alone." He wrapped her up and held her close.

Avery leaned into him. She'd come to Europe to forget her sorrows and put the past behind her. She'd never dreamed she would find her future and a home. "Maybe I never was." She leaned back and stared deeply into his eyes. "I don't think all of this could have happened without some help. Maybe my parents are still watching out for me."

"Christmas is a time for miracles."

"And angels." She smiled and kissed him lightly.

"Come—we will spend the morning opening presents, and then you will talk me out of eloping this afternoon."

She laughed easily. A thought suddenly hit her. "I want to start a tradition." She climbed out of the bed and dug into her backpack. "Well, it's not a new tradition for you, but it is for me, and I'd like to make it ours."

She made her way back to the bed and stood in front of him. He put his hands on her hips, and her knees melted. She tucked her wild hair behind her ear and lifted the box up for him to see. "This is, I hope, the first of many."

He took the box from her and opened the lid. Moving aside the wrapping, he found the string and pulled out the ornament she'd bought in Venice.

"I didn't know it when I bought it, but it's perfect for us." She lightly tapped the side, making a clicking sound with her nail. "It's blue and silver—your family's colors."

He nodded.

"But look, it has a set of turtledoves—like you and me. And they are flying together as if they just met." She suddenly felt shy and overly romantic. "I thought we could buy an ornament for our tree every year—one that represented the family we will be."

"I love it." He folded his hands carefully over hers. "And I love that you want to have a family with me. Tell me, love, how many children do you want to have?"

She blushed deeply. As much as it thrilled her to talk of these things with Matteo, it was also like baring her soul. "Three." She glanced up, hoping he wasn't disappointed or shocked.

His smile brightened the whole room. "The perfect number." He kissed her three times in quick succession. "Welcome home, Avery."

She smiled against his lips as the last kiss lingered. She was truly home in his arms. "Many years from now, when our grandchildren ask for the story of how we fell in love, I will tell them that it all started when I was snowed in at the castle."

He smiled. "And I will tell them that you fell in love with me because I twirled."

She giggled as he pulled her close and claimed her lips. She breathed him in, reveling in the spicy scent of his cologne and the feel of his broad shoulders under her hands. Real men twirled—oh yes, they did. And they kissed. And they loved. And they built a future and a family.

Avery had her man, and she couldn't have been happier.

To read the next Snowed in for Christmas novel, click here..

This story is an irresistible contemporary

romance about a not-so-humble cop who splits his raffle ticket with an unlucky waitress and the actor who falls in love with her.
(An *It Could Happen to You* retelling with a twist!)

You'll also be registered for Lucy's newsletter where you'll receive free delicious recipes and updates about her book releases.

Click here to receive your FREE gift.

EverDayLove!
The Great Christmas Contest
Christmas Magic

Billionaire Bachelor Cove
Her Beast of a Billionaire Boss
Her Awkward Blind Date with the Billionaire
Her Marriage Pact with the Billionaire

Dating Mr. Baseball
Delay of Game
Caught Looking
Intentional Walk
Heavy Hitter

Texas Titans Romances
The Miracle Groom
The Warrior Groom
The Guardian Groom
The Devout Groom

Or get all four football romances at a great price
and FREE on KU

Lucy's Football Collection

Billionaire Marriage Brokers

The Academic Bride
The Organized Bride
The Professional Bride
The Country Bride
The Protective Groom
The Resilient Bride
The Athletic Groom
The Corporate Groom

The Snow Valley Series

Welcome to Snow Valley, Montana, where
romance is always in season.
Blue Christmas
Love in Light and Shadow
Romancing Her Husband
Wedding Fever
One Date Deal
His Wedding Date Fake Fiancee

Echo Ridge Romances
For a small town in Up-state New York, Echo
Ridge has a great big heart.

The Candy Counter Heiress
The Lion, the Witch, and the Library
A Brand New Second Chance

While You Were Skiing
A Brandnew Ball Game

Or, get all four books at an amazing price and
FREE on KU
Echo Ridge Romance Collection

The Destination Billionaire Romance Series
Beautiful locations, handsome heroes, and
romance.

The Reclusive Billionaire
Royal Distraction

Collections
Great for binge reading!

Sports Romance Collection
Billionaire Romance Series Sampler
Billionaire Marriage Brokers Brides Collection

ABOUT THE AUTHOR

Lucy McConnell has always been a reader and a writer. She writes fantasy, clean romance, Christian romance, historical fiction, and cookbooks under the name Christina Dymock. When she's not writing, you can find her volunteering at the elementary school or the church; shuttling kids to baseball, soccer, basketball, or rodeo, depending on the time of year; skiing with her family; wake boarding; cycling; or curled up with a good book.

You can sign up for her newsletter by clicking here and can check out here website here: http://lucymcconnell.wordpress.com/